THE LIAR

The Liar is one of Martin A. Hansen's best known and most popular novels. Written in 1950, the story, taking place shortly after World War II, is told in the first person and concerns the inhabitants of a tiny island in the Danish archipelago. In this absorbing psychological novel, the author probes deeply into the mind of Johannes Vig, the local schoolmaster and a lonely figure, whose relationship with his fellow islanders is gradually revealed in the diary supposedly written at the time of the actual events. The story also lays bare the schoolmaster's self-doubt, and his weaknesses, but at the same time it professes the author's steadfast belief in the goodness of man and the inviolability of life. Martin A. Hansen's philosophical and ethical convictions also emerge as the story progresses. Throughout, the novel displays the author's skill at indirect communication, in the manner of the philosopher Søren Kierkegaard.

The Liar is an unusual book, a sensitive and thought-provoking tale, and a fine example of Hansen's narrative technique.

MARTIN A. HANSEN

Born in 1909, Hansen was brought up in a traditional rural community some thirty miles south of Copenhagen. His first novels are closely observed studies of farming life, but during the war he wrote a powerful allegory of the Nazi tyranny. He worked for many years as a devoted teacher, but after the war he lived by his pen. He died in 1955.

MARTIN A. HANSEN

The Liar

Translated from the Danish by
JOHN JEPSON EGGLISHAW
With an Introduction by
ERIC CHRISTIANSEN

QUARTET ENCOUNTERS

Quartet Books   London Melbourne New York

First published in Great Britain
by Quartet Books Limited 1986
A member of the Namara Group
27/29 Goodge Street, London W1P 1FD

British Library Cataloguing in Publication Data

Hansen, Martin A.
The liar.
I. Title
839.8'1372[F]   PT8175.H3/

ISBN 0–7043–3499–2

Reproduced, printed and bound in Great Britain
by Nene Litho and Woolnough Bookbinding
both of Wellingborough, Northants

INTRODUCTION

Martin Hansen was born in 1909 at Strøby, a village some thirty miles south of Copenhagen. His family were peasants, and he was brought up in a traditional rural community. He never tired of remembering the world of his boyhood, nor ever wholly overcame his distrust of the world outside it. Yet his perspective was wide, even from an early age.

His father, an impoverished smallholder, had been to school, sang in the choir, and read history books; his mother preferred poetry. A sympathetic schoolmaster encouraged Martin to think, and he would sit in the crown of a pollarded poplar studying an *Illustrated History of the World* and imagining the hanging gardens of Babylon spread out below him. In his mind's eye, he met Socrates pacing the by-roads. The educational drive of the previous century, when devoted teachers had brought culture to the people, had faltered somewhat by this time. The local community hall, where apostles of progress had lectured, had come down in the world, and now 'reeked of beer at one end, and of piss at the other', but the ideal of self-improvement survived, and young Hansen embraced it. He was fascinated by literature, and the bus and the bicycle took him out of the parish.

He also had to work with his hands. He was by no means the first Danish littérateur with a practical knowledge of ploughing and reaping, but he acquired these skills more thoroughly than most. He left school at thirteen, and served as a farm labourer for three years before gaining entry to a teachers' training-college at the small town of Haslev. This was an evangelical institution, but he was proof against religious enthusiasm and for a while adopted the newer seductions of Socialism, Darwinism, and atheism.

In 1930 he took the train to Copenhagen, and began his career as a teacher in the poor district of Nørrebro. He worked there for fourteen years, trying to civilize the boys from the slums which then surrounded the great cemetery of the Assistens church, where the masters of Danish literature lie buried amid the clamorous epitaphs of the old bourgeoisie from which most of them came. Some of his views on education may be gathered from the diary of Johannes Vig. Like Dickens, he believed that taxonomy was no substitute for 'orthe-riding, and tried to stimulate curiosity before everything else; hence the cover in front of the bird-case in Sandø schoolroom.

A photograph from the thirties shows a serious, stalwart young man at one with the pack of urchins ranged alongside him. In fact, he became a heavy smoker, a drinker and a sleepless hypochondriac. His marriage to Vera Jensen in 1935 gave him an anchor he sorely needed, and his first novel was published that year. *Nu opgiver han* (*Now He Surrenders It*) is a broad canvas of yokels in distress which follows the social-realist model, but concludes with a rejection of the revolutionary route to social justice. The Big House burns down, and the socialist rejoices; but the fire was started by a mere arsonist, for his own sexual gratification.

The book won fame as an account of a disintegrating rural society, and it was followed by *The Colony* (1937) which describes the failure of a rural utopian experiment. Hansen then concluded that the tradition of the realistic novel, which had flourished in Denmark since the turn of the century, had run its course. He believed that Naturalism was an erroneous doctrine, which emphasized immediacy and originality at the cost of ignoring 'the great human phenomena: guilt, responsibility, belief in God, in the Devil, sacrifice, love, ecstacy, to name a few. It cannot raise itself to the tragic, or liberate itself in the comic, in humour'.

He turned instead to the earlier tradition of the picaresque, and in 1941 published *Jonathan's Journey*, a Quixotic romance in which two fellow-travellers debate the condition of modern man, torn between two futilities, technocracy and reactionary nostalgia. The Devil allows them to realize their fantasies of a better world, and to witness the annihilation of these utopias. The domineering plutocrat was given the name of Alexander, later to be applied in malice to the Socialist engineer Harry in *The Liar*.

This view of the hopelessness of man's present condition was at first confirmed by the shame of the German occupation. But the national strike of summer 1944 restored Hansen's faith in his own people, and inspired him to join the Resistance movement. He published an illegal article, went into hiding, and survived until the Liberation in hospital, after a nervous collapse. Two young men who had been persuaded by his words to join the struggle were killed, and his responsibility for their deaths haunted him thereafter.

During the strike, he finished another picaresque historical novel, *Christopher the Fortunate* (*Den Lykkelige Kristoffer*) which recounts the last journey and martyrdom of a noble young knight during the meaningless civil wars of the 1530s. Sir Christopher's 'good fortune' was to die for something worthwhile: truth and justice. His companion, brother Martin, expresses a more sceptical view of life, but the author's sympathy lies with the other martyr, the monk Matthew, who stands for the old Catholic order. Respect for heroes never dwindled in Hansen, as his treatment of the polar explorers and the fisherman Erik in *The Liar* indicates.

After the war, he lived by his pen. He was committed to a religious point of view, which gave him what he found lacking in political organization and technological progress. He wrote that 'the Socialist battle against social injustice is not in vain, but is inadequate as a basis for life'. He also challenged the nationalist veneration for the Vikings, arguing that to idealize the pre-Christian cult of violence was much the same as pandering to the post-Christian tendency of Nazism. The only worthwhile inheritance from Nordic antiquity was a fundamental sense of justice, which he detected behind various religious systems, even if it was more fully realized in the Catholic Middle Ages. His search for spiritual roots drew him back in time, and one of his last published works, *Serpent and Bull* (*Orm og Tyr*, 1952) was a study of the religious thought of ancient Scandinavia. He expressed his concern with the problems of contemporary society in essays, short stories and the anti-materialist tract *Leviathan* (1950).

He moved into an old rectory near Lejre (associated with King Hrothgar of *Beowulf*), and lived there in failing health with his wife and two children from 1950. He travelled within the Nordic world, but never outside it; the Occupation had taught him enough about the forces which prevailed elsewhere. On a visit to Stockholm he drank some bleach by mistake, and fatally damaged his kidneys. Sickness prevented his finishing a new series of short stories, *The Conch* (*Konkylien*, 1955), and he died of uraemia in June 1955, at the age of forty-five.

According to *The Times Literary Supplement* (9 December 1955) his death 'robbed Danish literature of one of its most accomplished prose stylists'. The most stylish of his prose is perhaps to be found in the collections of stories which appeared in 1946 and 1947: *The Thorn Bush* (*Tornebusken*) and *The Partridge* (*Agerhønen*). Nevertheless, the most acclaimed of his works was a novel published after he had decided that this form of fiction was virtually obsolete. It was like the gruesome cat in the Norwegian folk tale, so he claimed. She swallowed the farmer and his wife, then the fox and the bear, then the bridal procession and the funeral, and finally the sun and moon. Then the goat butted her over the cliff and she burst. So the firm, capacious structure which had enabled great novelists to contain great ideas within this form had been stretched to breaking-point. Since 1945 'the poem, the play, and the short story wing overhead like wild fowl'. The would-be novels stay on the ground and flap their wings, like tame geese who cannot fly.

The Liar began soon after the war, as a short story to be called 'The Ice Breaks'. Then it became a radio play, broadcast in 1949, and was published the following year as a novel. It appeared as a film in 1970. Despite the author's misgivings, the tame goose takes off, lifted by the conflict between good and evil which occupies the devious and lonely mind of the narrator. Johannes Vig's diary for March 13–16 is a fiction, the island of Sandø is an allegory, and its flora, fauna and population are an infestation of symbols, let loose with an ironical smile by one who disliked symbolism, feared duplicity and asserted, through Vig, the primacy of scientific description over other varieties of art.

Vig is a liar trying to tell the truth. 'Don't pronounce that name too quickly,' he asks, because it will sound like Johannes Svig, 'the fraud'; but his credentials as a moralist are apparently genuine. He holds the office of deacon (*degn*), which normally carries with it the duties of parish clerk, but in the isolated community of Sandø also entails the schoolmastership, the postmastership and a sort of perpetual curacy, in lieu of the parish priest on the mainland. He writes of his relations with some fifteen living parishioners, several dead ones, a group of schoolchildren, over twenty varieties of bird and an awakening landscape. He has two confidants: the imaginary reader Nathanael and the Gordon Setter Pigro, whom he trusts 'next to God' because he shares his animal nature. Shooting and philandering are his passions, but he finds happiness in neither, and in the end suggests that the whole book is an elegy for the faithful dog.

Vig, unlike Pigro, is tormented by conscience. His dealings with the islanders, especially with Annemari and Rigmor, the women who attract him, are usually playful and evasive, but not seriously dishonest. 'No, I'm not telling the truth,' he warns them. The men he mistrusts, Harry the Socialist engineer and Frederik the rich farmer, are also men he respects. He is devoted to the children, and feels that the schoolroom itself 'forgives him', since there his work justifies his existence. Outside, his attempts to do the right thing are less successful. Nevertheless, despite his drinking, philandering and moping, he conducts a sort of spring campaign against the Devil, timed to coincide with the arrival of the woodcock.

In Vig's theology, the Devil wins when men cease to find meaning in life, and surrender in mind, as in body, to the power of death. Godlessness leaves man defenceless. All forms of benevolent materialism enthrone death in the cause of progress. According to the Gospel for the third Sunday in Lent, Luke xi 14–28, which Vig reads to his flock, the unclean spirit driven out of man's soul (by God), will return with reinforcements unless the soul receive God in his place. As he reads, he feels the presence of Beelzebub, urging him to preach, that is, to promote optimism through fiction. He remains silent, fortified by the words of a widow who has learned to face death. After this experience, his morals remain as untidy as his house, but he recognizes that if he 'cannot grow', he 'can fight', because 'when you reach the limits of meaninglessness, you find that all is a battleground, where two forces fight, and there isn't any no man's land'. His contribution to the battle consists of not taking Rigmor from her husband, but receiving into his house a pregnant and unwanted barmaid. He also renounces fiction in favour of topography. The pain of thwarted love confirms his faith. 'I know God's presence only when he strikes me hard,' he claims. However, his obtuseness is also penetrated by a sense of the spiritual worth of other islanders.

The book is both a vindication of religious truth and a farewell to the traditional modes of extended fiction. It is haunted by literary ghosts, and English readers will recognize the shadowy forms of Hans Andersen (there is even a little Kay to be carried off by the Snow Queen) and Søren Kierkegaard, 'the greatest Christian thinker of modern times' in Hansen's opinion. The most genial of the tutelary spirits of Sandø appears to be Sten Blicher, the sporting parson from Jutland, who launched the Danish tradition of prose fiction in 1824 with an earlier *Diary of a Parish Clerk* (*En Landbydegns Dagbog*), cramming the substance of a long historical romance into the compass of an imaginary journal. There is hardly a foible or a frailty in Johannes Vig which was not to be found in Blicher himself, from his addiction to the gun and the bottle to his passion for ornithology, music and topography, his slovenliness, his debts, his dogs and his veneration for one fairly insignificant hill.

Much has been written about Hansen since his death, and many of his works have been translated into English, mainly in journals and anthologies. The most convenient monograph, which includes a full bibliography, is *Martin A. Hansen* by Faith and Niels Ingwersen (Twayne Publishers, Boston, 1976).

Eric Christiansen
Oxford 1986

THE LIAR

Map of Sandö

I

THIRTEENTH of March. It is foggy.

I have a feeling I want to tell you something, Nathanael. Nothing very much: only I must talk to someone for a while.

It is the thirteenth of March, Nathanael, and Friday.

There is fog outside, and although still early afternoon, it is so dark in my room that I can hardly see what I am writing. But then, what I write is of little importance.

Thirteenth of March. Fog.

We have had fog before, while the ice has surrounded the island, but not this mild, wet fog, Nathanael. I was up before dawn this morning, and discovered that fog had set in over the island during the night. The trees in the garden loom coal-black, but I can only faintly discern my spruce trees at the bottom of the garden.

Can it really be spring? Touch wood!

If it is spring, there's going to be unrest in the hearts of the people on Sandö, and that is what I am afraid of, Nathanael.

> Here are hearts in plenty,
> Here are ten for one,
> Hearts for hearts abounding,
> Were they kind each one
> Yet if this I trusted,
> All the game might rue,
> If the nine play falsely,
> Only ace be true.
> Gamble not on hearts, friend,
> Think how oft the cost

Has been paid when others
played in hearts—and lost.

So runs the warning of Ambrosius Stub.

Thirteenth of March, and a fog, so thick you might stir it
with a ladle, completely hides the island of Sandö. The
island itself is only two miles long and one mile broad, but
fog covers the ice, too, and that lies for miles beyond and
around the island. The ice has closed us in for forty years.
For forty years.

A man, too, can perhaps be such an island.

Drops of water falling from the roof gleam in the light.
And look! A flock of sparrows are celebrating a betrothal
in one of the bushes: that's a good sign.

It is so dark in here that I nearly said I couldn't see what
I was saying! But of course, I am writing, Nathanael, writing whatever comes into my head. Though it is possible
that I am talking to myself—it's a habit one gets. I am never
aware of it, until I hear something beating softly against
the wall by the stove. It's my dog, Pigro, lying in his box
and wagging his tail. He looks up at me, and I realize
that I've been talking to myself again.

I let the children out of school early today because of
the fog. They couldn't keep still for a moment—not that
we grownups are any better! "You can go! Out with you!
It is spring!"

Better touch wood!

At least, it is the thaw. The ice drips and oozes and
fidgets. From down along the shore, I can hear the youngsters shouting with joy. Listen!

If spring has really come, there'll be a heap of trouble
here on Sandö. The world is drift sand, and the sand
blinds our eyes. Spring brings nothing but trouble. When
the ice breaks and the sea is open again, a lot will happen,

one way and another. You will have plenty to think about, Annemari: this engineer fellow, Alexander, will go away; and what then, Annemari? Oluf will come home again; and what then, Annemari?

Why should I care? "It doesn't concern us two, does it, Pigro? No, we are just waiting for the woodcock, Pigro, waiting for the birds of passage." We ourselves are birds of passage.

"Can you hear, Pigro, how the children shout and scream down on the beach?" They sound just like a flock of birds coming in. I shouldn't wonder if they are playing on the ice, despite my warning.

You see, Nathanael, I can't very well talk to the walls of my room, or the bookshelves, or the dust on the table, not even to Pigro, though he is an exceptional dog. "Dear me, you'll soon be old, Pigro! Not so many years are left for our outings together." Never have I seen a better dog for woodcock. "I hope we meet again on the other side and go shooting together, Pigro."

So I have come to need you, Nathanael, just to listen to me. I don't really know who you are, I only call you "Nathanael" because it is said that Nathanael was a man without guile. I fancy you are not so clever and sophisticated as I am, although I'm only as blasé as the times in which I live. Imagining you as open and sincere, I think of you as a friend I might have met in my youth, but never did, and that you have grown no older. I had friends once, but I have lived so long on an island, they have forgotten me, Nathanael—it's only natural.

I ought, I suppose, to introduce myself. I am, God help me, the schoolmaster on Sandö, a molehill in the sea: a bachelor, and beginning to go thin on the top. My name is Johannes Vig. Don't pronounce that name too quickly, Nathanael—"Johannes Vig."

I have nothing important to tell you, only I have a feeling there's going to be a lot of trouble on Sandö, that something is about to take place. I would rather say "take place" than "happen." Granted the island is small, a molehill in a field of blue, what are its problems compared with the problems of the great world outside? Nothing. But then, how great are the problems of the world when viewed from Orion's Belt, Nathanael?

I have certainly pondered the problems of the great world, Nathanael, and I think I even understand them a little, but I dare say you can do without my ideas on that subject, my friend.

Hear how they yell! They should be careful now—new holes may appear in the ice. I ought to go down there.

So it is spring again, or soon will be. What then? This engineer, Alexander, will go away and Oluf will come home again, and what then, Annemari? "But that has nothing to do with us two, Pigro; we are only waiting for the woodcock."

Listen! I really ought to go down and give an eye to the children.

There was little to see on the ice yesterday, no new holes had appeared. I was out towards evening with my gun and Pigro. The sea ice was rough and its pores were open; but it has been like that for a long time. The only change was that the ice was sweating more. I was over by the large openings to the northwest, where I thought I might come within range of a brent-goose. There have been one or two of these birds among the others for a week or so now. Not that I would shoot. These poor winter birds are not protected, but they are so miserably thin now, for the sea has been frozen over for six weeks. It would be very easy to shoot eider duck, tufted duck, razor bill, black guillemot, merganser, and several others, but to what purpose? I took the gun just in case I saw a seal.

Flocks of birds flew up from the holes. I counted nine wild geese. So the wild geese are here already! I scattered some corn on the ice edge and threw some pieces of bread into the water. Only the sea ducks will take it in the water and they must teach the others—the black scoter, the tufted and the long-tailed duck—to eat bread. You can stand and watch them through field glasses.

I should like to take you with me for a couple of days, Nathanael, on one of my shore hunts. You might get a touch of rheumatism through getting wet and lying under cover on the ice, but you would learn to understand the fleeting life of the earth. Wild life comes and goes quickly, but is of the same stuff and nature as our own. Do you know the fleeting life of a flower or a blade of grass, Nathanael? Have you ever looked into the eye of a large wild bird as you took aim over the foresight, Nathanael? Say the eye of a wild goose? If you have, you will know that she is a fugitive from your own heart.

But I was going down to look after the children.

Instead, I sit here waiting for Annemari to come with the coffee. She said she would come herself this morning, as she wanted to talk to me about something. Indeed!

I wonder if she'll come? It's long past her time. I am not so sure that I want her to come, either, particularly when she has something special she wants to talk about. That means trouble, I know. Whenever anyone on the island says to me: "I have something I should like to talk to you about, sir!" I know it means trouble. Something to occupy my mind and keep me awake at night, though it is no concern of mine. People have minds like tangled yarn: they come to me with their tangles and I know neither where to begin nor where to end.

I get lots of trouble, but I don't take it too seriously, Nathanael. I just say what comes easiest. Perhaps I feel like a passenger on a train, who, getting out for a moment at a station, is asked this and that by a lot of people; but being on a journey, he is thinking of other things and cannot take it too seriously.

Now I cannot see the spruce trees at the bottom of the garden at all. Those lovely spruce trees that screen me from the ever present view of the monotonous island and the everlasting sea when I sit here in my room.

But listen! There's not a sound coming from the ice now. Only drip, drip from the roof.

I realize now that it is some time since I heard any sound from the children. Strange! I wonder if anything has happened? Fiddlesticks! It's just that they have gone home. "No, Pigro, stay where you are!"

I am sitting in the half-light writing in a new notebook, Nathanael. The paper smells fine. I have had it all the winter. During the autumn, when I made a trip to the mainland, I bought a whole pile of these books. I meant to buy no more than two, because two last me a year. I bought twenty. That's just like me. I was thinking of the long winter evenings here alone. But the books have lain unused all the winter, and only today have I begun to write in one of them.

On the shelf, right in front of me, so that I can always see them, stands a long row of notebooks which I have filled in the course of time. There must be at least a score of them. The ink is fading and their backs are turning yellow. I never touch them, and I should never dream of looking in them again. All the same, there is a deal of good stuff in them. I have made copious notes on Sandö's fishing, its weather, its vegetation, and its birds.

There's not a sound. The ice holes! Something may have happened.

"Up with you, Pigro! We must go and see."

"Not so crazy, Pigro! This way, through the kitchen. We must take some crumbs for the ducks."

But look! What has been going on here? Here's the coffee on the kitchen table—cold! Annemari has been here, but she didn't come into the room. She had somewhere else to go, she has so much to do nowadays. She is Dido and must stay close to her Aeneas, this engineer. But he will be going away soon; and what then, Annemari? Your sweetheart, Oluf, is coming home again; and what then, Annemari?

In the garden, under the pear tree, the eranthis are already out. They have appeared so suddenly they quite take my breath away. One—two—three! They spread their green skirts and curtsy. "Welcome, eranthis!"

"This way, Pigro, over the fields."

I hope nothing has happened.

Oh, thank goodness! I can hear some of them playing farther away, over by the quayside. "We must go down and see them, Pigro."

I do believe I was quite worried about them. I am quite hot.

Yes, but one gets hot walking over plowed fields; and this fog, too, it is so mild. One's boots become twice their size walking on soil so soft and heavy. There is only a little snow left in the furrows. "Take a good look at that snow, Pigro. Like a dog's guilty conscience, isn't it?"

Here is the road, covered with large pools, but there is nothing for them to reflect, only the fog. As I walk, my heavy boots make scarcely a sound, only "sjip, sjip."

Pigro skips off into the ditch and splashes about. His long coat curls up and his fantail wags. A good hunter and a fine pointer. A Gordon setter, but not quite pure-bred. Pigro is black enough, muddy black on the head and back, but, poor fellow, he has only one light spot on his breast where he should have two.

Hallo! He has flushed a bird. A lark? Surely not. Quiet! Yes, I can hear it somewhere in the fog. True enough, it's a young lark borne on the southern winds.

What now, Annemari?

One cannot rely on larks or eranthis or even one's feelings. Winter is an old warrior and may return. It would perhaps be better if it did, for spring brings nothing but turmoil. Spring comes, and perhaps one of our old folks must say good-bye. Spring means only confusion and trouble.

We could quite easily have waited. Granted, things are running short at the shop: he has only the worst of the bottled stuff left, I know that. But it would do. Newspapers? We never miss them. Letters? They are only a worry, and I never receive any. The parish clerk on Sandö is forgotten by everyone he ever knew.

Stop! Pigro has taken up position. A beautiful, fixed stance. "Fine, fine, old boy! We can do it, Pigro." Dead still! You can hear a withered blade of grass straighten after shedding a drop of dew.

Forward!

Bllullull!

Two partridges fly away into the fog. And I stand here like a fool, holding my stick like a gun in the air. "It's spring, Pigro, spring! The birds are in pairs now."

There is no sign of children by the burial mound or along the dike, and I can see for some distance out over the mildewed sea ice. There's a lot of surface water, and it's turning dark, but there is no one here.

We follow the dike. Long pearl necklaces of dew fall on

Pigro from the old mugwort. Now there is a smell of smoke and tar; and soon a red glow in the fog ahead. Black shapes move around the glow: Robert and his sons have a fire under the tar-kettle and are busy boiling their nets. Steam and smoke cloud up into the fog, and the hot air above the kettle quivers. The men fairly shine with tar, and here are all the children flocking round. They are in good hands.

"Hush, Pigro, we will slip away. Let us go for a walk to the Sand Hills. Come then! No? You want to go and see little Tom? All right, we'll go and see little Tom."

At Höst's, the shop is chock-full. All men. Fishermen and oil, small-holders and leather, salted herrings, cheese, damp woolens, and tobacco smoke make a good mixture. Lord, how they jabber! About the fog and the spring, and the spring and the fog.

The half deaf grocer, Höst, and his assistant serve. Annemari is nowhere to be seen, but little Tom is here. Pigro retrieves him from behind the counter. "Hallo, little Tom!" He is munching sweets, of course. His grandfather spoils him. I sit on the sacks and lift him on to my knee. "What do you think, Tom? Pigro and I have seen two partridges. When they get chicks, we three will go out and find them. You should see how the old birds look after their young. When it rains or is cold, all the chicks hide under the two birds, and you would think that father and mother were afloat, bobbing up and down on a wave of chicks."

Here comes Annemari.

She doesn't notice us, but she nods to the group of men, a sweet and precious nod, then walks by with downcast eyes. Annemari has curved, black eyelashes, and seen in profile she is just a child. But she is mother to Tom here, and her thick woolen blouse cannot hide her womanhood.

31

The Rose of Sandö. But look! Annemari is wearing ski pants. She never dresses like this when she comes to see me: I wonder why? Stop wondering, schoolmaster! you are getting too old. Annemari's cheeks are red as fire, not with the weather but with the laughter and fun she is having in the warm room behind the shop. Can it be that she has a visitor in there? A cigarette is held gracefully between two fairly yellow fingers. I have noticed that you have lovely yellow fingers lately, Annemari. I wonder how many films you saw when you were staying over in the town? These movements as you climb the little ladder and reach up to the shelf for some cigarettes, and that pretty behind there for all the men to see! It's the films, my girl. Look here, you're getting too old, parish clerk!

Annemari has gone.

"Annemari is beautiful," says one.

"Annemari is a snipe," says another.

The grocer is half deaf, so they don't bother about him.

"Would you like to come home with me, little Tom?" I ask aloud. The men stop talking and smile. But Tom will not come today, not until I, to my shame, entice him with sweets. Outside, Pigro goes quite crazy, dancing about in slush and licking the child. Tom cannot stand it today, he begins to cry and wants to go home to his mother and the engineer. "Do you like the engineer, Tom?" "Oh, yes, yes!" So I have to let Tom go back into the shop.

"Look here, Pigro! You must take more care another time! Yes, I admit people are difficult to understand."

The day goes at last, and darkness gathers.

It is freshening a little outside, and as I sit in the dark, peering out, the fog swirls past the windows like an army of ghosts.

Annemari herself is coming with my evening meal. "Are you there, Johannes?" she asks, standing in the doorway.

32

I wait a while, holding the sound of her voice in my ear, before I answer: "No!"

I light the lamp and draw the blinds.

Annemari sits down at the table opposite to me. I am so used to eating alone that I sometimes find it immodest to do it in front of others. Like the owls. But it doesn't worry Annemari, she just sits quietly while I eat. She can sit so naturally in my room without speaking.

Annemari has black eyelashes, rose-red lips, a red coral necklace, and a moss-green blouse. If that doesn't sound good, it doesn't look bad. She is wearing a skirt now.

She sits fiddling with one of my pens, an old, thin one, plain but almost sacred. I would never give it away, but I might consider leaving it to somebody in my will. "Go on, break it, my girl," think I, "then I shall light the fire with it tomorrow, or plant the pieces in a flowerpot. If it grew leaves and flowers I could be sure there was some truth in my notebooks."

"Are you coming to the dance on Sunday night?" she asks.

"There's a dance?"

"They are holding the spring festival at the Headlands on Sunday. You once promised you would dance a whole night with me, Johannes."

"Too late, too late, Annemari. I'm getting too old."

"You're jesting. You should go. And then. . . ."

"And then what, Annemari?"

"Well . . . you could meet Harry. I think you would like him. He'll be going away soon."

"So it's Harry you call the engineer, and here have I been calling him Alexander."

"Why did you call him Alexander?"

"Yes, I wonder why, my girl? Never mind, you have someone to dance with now."

"I believe you would like Harry, Johannes."

"I don't doubt it for a moment; but tell me, aren't you going to dance away from the island?"

"Say straight out what you mean!" she said, and looked at me with a spark in each eye. "You mean that I'm dancing away with the engineer, with Harry, that is what you mean!"

"My imagination was not so fertile, my girl. But if you do dance over to the mainland, give my regards to Oluf."

She threw the pen down and exclaimed: "That was a strange thing for you to say!"

"Was it strange? When I have a chance I send my regards to Oluf. I am his friend, maybe the only one he has, besides you, of course."

Silence. What was that? Just a fly near Pigro. He snaps at it, half asleep.

"Can you hear a fly?" she asks.

"No!" I answer.

"You once knew a girl you couldn't forget, Johannes."

"Have I told you that, Annemari? Who can it be? Aase, perhaps?"

"You have never mentioned that name before."

"Forgive me, I get mixed up, Annemari, and mistake one for another. It's all so long ago, generations ago."

"The one for whose sake you came out here to Sandö?"

"That was you, Annemari!"

"You are always joking. You didn't know me, besides I was only sixteen."

"Reports about the Rose of Sandö travel far, my dear. I came, I saw, I was conquered—unfortunately."

"Why 'unfortunately'?"

"A schoolmaster cannot very well be in love with his young pupil. It would only lead to harm, and could never bring happiness. Then, a year later, you came and introduced Oluf to me."

34

"Why didn't you run away with me? Did you never think about that?"

"I have never thought about anything else. Will you run away with me now?"

"Right now?" she said. "You are always jesting, and about everything, Johannes."

"As a matter of fact I never jest," I said, "but what was it you wanted to know about the girl of whom you were speaking? Birte was her name."

"There, you see," she said, "last time you called her Betty. I do believe you have made it all up."

"That is the disadvantage of invention, my dear, one can never tell the same story twice."

"I believed it all the same," she said, and simply plowed the pen through my blotting-pad. "You once got a necklace from her, you said."

"From Betty? Did I tell you that?" I asked; her question seemed to suggest I had stolen it.

"Lend it to me!" said Annemari. She looked at me with eyes full of fire.

"You would like to borrow it?"

"To wear at the dance on Sunday!" she answered. And how her eyes shone!

"Of course, what a good idea!"

The fly buzzed round again. I ought to kill it. It can breed millions more, and during the summer Sandö is black with flies.

"Then lend it to me!" she said. "Strange," I thought. So I had to search round to see where the necklace might be.

"It should be here in this drawer, but I don't see it."

"Have you looked carefully, Johannes?"

"It isn't here, but I will look somewhere else, my dear."

"No, don't bother."

"I wonder if it is raining?" I said. It was certainly blowing harder.

"It will not be long now!" she said. She was looking straight ahead and her eyes were shining.

I moved my hand in the direction of the bookshelf and asked: "Would you like me to read you something tonight?"

"No, thank you," she answered.

"It's getting colder outside," I said after we had sat for a while.

"Either you have been telling me lies, or you don't want to lend me that necklace!"

"Then I must have been telling lies, Annemari."

"I must go now," she said.

"You have been here a long time," I said; "perhaps you have company at home?"

She shook her head and looked absorbed.

"The wind is getting up," I said, "the ice will break. Oluf will be coming home."

"Stop it!" she screamed.

This time she flung the pen on the floor, and the nib stuck in the floorboards near Pigro. The dog lay with his head on the edge of his box and watched the pen quivering.

I nodded and smiled at her. She looked lovely, intensely alive, a flower just burst into life.

"Stop it!" she said again, but quite softly this time.

"Forgive me," she murmured, and then strode out leaving the door open. I walked over to the steps and watched her go. The wind was not as strong as it had seemed indoors. All the snow had gone now, and it was quite dark.

I sat in my room for some time in the dark and looked out at the black row of spruce trees. But it was no good. I lit the lamp and took a stiff cognac. There were only three or four small glasses left in the bottle—my last—and I knew I was in for some restless, sleepless nights. "Yes, Pigro, old fellow, things look bad."

II

FOURTEENTH of March. Saturday morning.

It is half past six and daylight. I am sitting in the schoolroom where I lit the stove an hour ago. The sweet smell of turf smoke hangs about the room, and the heat of the stove is beginning to reach my table. The schoolroom is cosy, not very large, only sixteen feet by twenty-three. I have the lamp lit, though there is plenty of light coming in from the south windows, a cold blue light. Through the west windows I can see the day-moon fading behind the clouds above Western Hill.

The schoolroom is still fairly dismal. Some years ago I had Rasmus Sandbjerg paint the high wainscot with a ground color and decorate it with a flower design in the old style that he had inherited years before. Rasmus was a very old man when he painted it, and he died of contentment with his work.

I like to sit by myself in the schoolroom of a morning. One becomes a slightly different person by being here.

What was it I called you last night? Oh, yes! "Nathanael!" I had to have someone to talk to, so I called you in from some place or other. But now I think there is something queer about it. In the morning one is perhaps not quite the same as at night. Who knows? Perhaps I am not exactly the same when I sit among the books and instruments in my own room, where, through the window, I see only the overgrown garden and the lovely dark spruce trees. I mean that I can perhaps become somewhat different here in the schoolroom. It may be so. I am just a little self-conscious about what I told you last night, Nathanael.

I think that, for the moment, I imagined you were my son. What nonsense! If I had a son, I should tell him about other people, about plants and birds, and about all the fleeting things of the earth; but never about myself.

I am sitting here waiting for the children, but they won't arrive for nearly two hours. Then there'll be an odor of wet mittens, dubbin, and smoked sausages. Let me tell you about the children, Nathanael. There are thirteen in the older class, which comes today, and sixteen in the younger class, which was here yesterday. Thirteen little men and women, thirteen strange creatures, and here sits a fourteenth. Don't you think we are strange, Nathanael? I don't mean only mentally, but in every way. Have you never really marveled at those peculiar mussel shells of gristle we have on each side of our heads, I mean our ears? Or look at your hand, Nathanael. Move your fingers and watch them closely. Are they not strange?

I have no intention of being profound or philosophical about it, yet as a visitor here on earth one must learn to marvel. What can I say when I walk among the flowers in the fields? Words cannot convey very much. Have we fleeting souls any lasting place other than in the moment in which we marvel at existence? But don't ponder over this too much, Nathanael.

I like to sit in the morning before the children come, and wonder at one thing or another. It's a kind of technique. I call it my wonder-hour, and it can be very useful. I sit at ease and get useful little ideas and suggestions that are good for a teacher.

Nothing happened to the ice during the night. After midnight the wind coming from the northwest slackened until it was only slight when Pigro and I went for a walk towards the Sand Hills. The night was clear and the moon was up. It has just been full moon. As I stood on the hill, the island lay below me like a dark black boat. Round about it lay the ice, luminous, as if there was phosphorus in it.

There was frost in the air, and I could hear the birds quarreling in the ice holes. Some swans came flying in, I could hear their singing, "Yim, yim, yim!" A flock of widgeon passed over, too.

I cannot sleep at nights again. The cognac didn't help at all, and that's why I creep like a ghost round the sleeping island.

Last night I sat and thought about Annemari and why she wanted to borrow the necklace. She came to borrow a necklace, a trinket, that's what she came for yesterday. Now is it like Annemari to want to borrow something? I shouldn't have thought so. But she would borrow a necklace to wear at the spring dance at the Headlands tomorrow. Why? Because it's the last time she'll be with this engineer? The ice is breaking and he'll go away, and what then, Annemari? Oluf will come home, and what then, Annemari?

How she lost her temper when I mentioned Oluf, even though she is betrothed to him and he is little Tom's father! She flew into a passion and threw my pen on the floor. She looked lovely, like a lapwing that flies at you straight between the eyes. She has eyelashes that are remarkably black.

No, she wouldn't hear me speak of Oluf. The pen is still sticking in the floor, and I had better get it out of the way before Margrete does her Saturday cleaning, or she'll begin to wonder.

But I didn't worry myself so very much last night about the necklace and Annemari. I am no longer so crazy about solving puzzles and finding explanations. As one grows older one learns to take things as they are, and Annemari is one of those little mysteries one fortunately comes across, something to marvel at a little.

Although I can't have had more than a couple of hours of sleep all night, I got up this morning as usual as soon as the alarm rang at half past four. I took a drop cognac before breakfast, I felt so out of sorts. That helped. But perhaps it's not a good thing to do. Yet it's very necessary for me to keep to my hours with almost military precision, otherwise it would soon spell ruin.

I went for a morning walk with Pigro in the garden. It was dark and misty, and there was hoarfrost; the little eranthis looked like rococo ladies with powdered hair. We went at a good pace down to the dike and then to the quayside. There was only frost and ice everywhere; the boats either lay up on land or were frozen in alongside the pier. All was silent.

It has been silent on the island for the last forty mornings, there has not been the sound of the motors from the cutters. A painful silence settled over Sandö when the ice formed round the island. There was the accident to Erik and the young fellow who was with him. The young man didn't belong to Sandö, he was from the mainland; but it was no easier for me that he was a stranger, for it was my job to ring over to the mainland to tell them he had been blown up and we had found nothing left of him, nor of Erik either.

Erik was the last and only one who dared go out with the cutter after the ice had closed the main current. He would go over to the town, and of course he had errands there for most of us. The young fellow would go home. It was dark and there was a frost-mist about when they set out that morning. We could hear them, now and then, lying out there cutting themselves free. Then we heard the motor away to the south of the island, and we could not quite understand what they were up to. It was about ten o'clock when it happened. I was in the schoolroom here with the children, when it made the windows rattle. Two of Erik's children were with me. That was the last of Erik and the young man. They had apparently tried to slip out of the ice pack over by the end of The Hook, and the mine had been lying in wait there. How else can it have happened? They never returned to tell us. We found only some splinters and the propeller shaft, which were thrown up on the Gysand reef.

Erik was our best man on Sandö. I do not forget that it was Erik who was first to go out to help when things went wrong for Oluf and Niels. They were another pair who dared to go out. Oluf and Niels capsized in a gale. Niels remained out there, Oluf came home. He swam more than two miles in the storm, and everybody talked about it for days. One almost forgets that Niels was there and lost his life. Niels was a quiet lad. Even in memory he is so quiet that one almost forgets him.

Yes, Erik was the first to go out that time, the first to help. Erik was short and dark—not like a viking—yet he always took the lead.

It is little more than a month ago we heard the mine explode. God help me that I should be parish clerk on Sandö! It fell to me to arrange the service, the priest from Tulö couldn't get here. And all that was left of Erik and the youth was the propeller shaft. Robert is a stout man, heavy, and crocus-blue over most of his face, but from the middle of his forehead upwards he is white: this is due to his cap, which he never takes off, even when he comes to see me. He did this time. But I understood why Robert took his cap off; the reason was his own serious thoughts.

"You think perhaps we ought to do something in the church?" I asked.

"Yes, that's what we were thinking," said Robert.

It was dusk and he stayed for a while, but without speak-

41

ing. I sat and thought to myself: "You have experienced this before. A man's nearest friend has been killed, and he sits here and would like to say something, but cannot. And you don't help him." I didn't remember if I really had experienced it before, but I came to think about the preacher's words: "That which hath been is that which shall be; and that which is done is that which shall be done, and there is no new thing under the sun."

We arranged for Wednesday, four o'clock in the church.

Yes, you are the withered leaf that the wind blows, and the wind has blown you into the church choir vault. You stand under the choir arch and look down at them. Their faces are turned towards you; pale heads above the rows of dark pews. Frost glistens on the mouldy church walls. Annemari sits erect on the organ seat and stares into the shifting light which burns by the side of the music. She ought to turn now and look towards you, but she doesn't. There below sits Lena, Erik's widow, and her three children. They all wait. Dead still in the clammy church. Waiting for you.

What have you to say to them?

I put out the lamp in the schoolroom. It is after half past seven. I heard Margrete arrive and I have forgotten to pick up the pen.

Yes, I like to sit in the schoolroom in the morning. I say to myself: "It is going to be a good day, a fine day, a surprising day! Now what can I think of?"

I like to hit upon something new in the morning: something for the children—a surprise to hang up on the wall, a new picture; but it must be done in a way that awakens their curiosity. It can be done even with the dull pictures that are produced for use in schools. I hang up such a picture with a cloth in front of it, so that it is hidden. I let it hang like that throughout the day. What happens? One of

42

the children peeps on the sly under the cover and during the interval they all look at it carefully. Once they are looking at it, we can talk about it.

Another day, an ordinary wood saw hangs by a string from the roof. It hangs unmentioned, until we are ripe for the centuries of ingenuity and experience there are in a wood saw. Fish nets, traps, parts of a plowshare, tools, pots and pans festoon the walls, often hidden under a cloth at first, until wonder is awakened over the beauty of such ordinary things.

Forgive me that I boast a little about these tricks, Nathanael; I can just as easily have my doubts.

When I came here the lower parts of the windows were whitewashed over. It must have disturbed my predecessor to see the children craning their necks to look out. I cleaned the whitewash off. Now, of course, I get the same trouble, but I firmly believe that they could not look at anything more important to them than what they see looking out of the windows here. In this landscape their memories will grow. Yet I often wonder if they look at it only because they have to sit in school. When they are playing outside they never see it.

The two windows face south. From them one looks down over the fields towards the dike and the Mound. Farther to the east lie the quayside and the lighthouse, while westwards the island rises towards the solitary hill in the south, on which the church is built, and towards Western Hill and the Mill Bank.

But it is towards the sea they look mainly, towards Golö. It was out there that Oluf and Niels capsized, and Niels never returned.

As long as I am here, I will try to spin fine threads about them and do my best to teach them to know their island, its earth, shore, birds, flowers, and all its changing life.

43

Some of them will leave Sandö, but perhaps the memory of the island will never leave them. I sit here and instil a delicate poison, so that my hold over them lasts a long time. But perhaps it is a hindrance nowadays to have roots in a place? I wonder.

I wonder how Oluf and Annemari would have fared? As youngsters they would have liked to leave the island. At one time they had great plans and were determined to be off. They are still here, however. Oluf is working at a factory over in the town for the winter, but will be back as soon as the sea is open, that's certain. Then he will go fishing, occasionally, or will sit on a bench, smoking his pipe and gazing out over the water. Indoors he will sometimes play his violin to be excused from talking. That's how it is with Oluf now.

Now that Oluf is coming home and the engineer is going away, what will Annemari do?

Oluf and Annemari came to my evening school, one of the first winters I was here. Niels was there, too, and about a dozen others. Annemari and Oluf sat together at the back, or rather she sat there and he had to follow. Oluf, the fair, big fellow—and he is prodigiously big—was as red as a beetroot and never lifted his eyes. He would move out to the very edge of the seat, then Annemari would pull him closer to her. She was seventeen, he eighteen. There has never been a more handsome couple.

Annemari was the most intelligent of them all. The next was Niels. Oluf was slower, but he was musical. The two of them came regularly, almost every night. I used to play music with Oluf and read books with Annemari. She went over to the mainland and took her preliminary examination, after which she was away for a good while taking a commercial course. What use was that to her here? Yes, they had plans, but Oluf got out of step and became slower. Then, also, Annemari was going to have a baby. Strangely

44

enough she would have it—little Tom—but even that didn't rouse Oluf. It was at the time that Niels was drowned that Oluf grew drowsy, as we know him now. What happened about their marriage and their plans? Nothing. It is a strange story, that of Oluf and Annemari, a sad little story.

"Pity I didn't find that necklace last night!" I said, when Annemari herself came with my dinner again.

"It was a silly idea of mine," she answered.

She spoke gently enough but without her usual familiarity.

At length, I thanked her for the dinner, got up, walked quickly to the door, and opened it. I thought so.

"You can make the coffee, Margrete!" I said.

Of course, the woman was standing just outside the door, listening with her ear to the keyhole. Perhaps she may control her curiosity now.

Annemari took a letter from her woolen blouse. When a girl has a bosom like Annemari's, it must be good to be such a letter—and be a good letter.

"Will you post this?" she asked. "I forgot to give it to you last night."

"It shall be done!" I answered in my capacity as postmaster on Sandö, but the arrival—and departure—of mail is not so regular here, as Miss Annemari was perhaps aware.

"The ice is breaking now," she said, "but read it! It is not sealed."

"I would rather not."

"You must," she insisted; "perhaps you have seen to whom it is addressed?"

"Yes, I have seen, my girl."

"I want you to read it."

"And I don't want to."

"I don't know what I shall do if you don't read it," she

45

threatened, and she came so close to me that I could feel that she was shaking from head to foot. "Perhaps there are some spelling mistakes!" she almost shouted.

I read the letter.

"There are no spelling mistakes," I said.

"And other mistakes?" she prompted. Annemari was calmer now, or pretended to be. How this girl could stare! Her head was thrown back, and her dark hair in disorder. Round her eyes was a dark fringe, like eyelashes after tears, but Annemari's eyelashes are always like that, though she rarely cries. At first sight, one is almost repulsed by this black velvet circle about the dark gray eyes, but not afterwards. There stood Annemari and stared. It ought to be a punishable offense for a girl to look like that.

I drew my breath and said: "Yes, there is a mistake."

"What mistake?" she asked. She looked guilty.

"The letter itself is a mistake," I answered; "but perhaps it is possible to make out a receipt in full for five or six years of love? One—two—three, a little receipt to the child's father. One—two—three—and good-bye, Oluf!"

"You don't understand," she said.

"I should refuse to, even if I could," I replied; "but are you sure you are doing the right thing?"

"Yes," she answered.

"Then there is no more to say," I said. "I will see to your letter. But perhaps the addressee will have left before the letter gets there. I think Oluf Olufsen will be here as soon as he can."

"That doesn't matter," she said. "At least, that's not what matters most. And I don't suppose he'll be very surprised by it, either."

I looked at her. How like a wild rose—even to the thorns! Annemari had always been resolute, but there was something here that made me suspicious. I wondered if she was not being prompted by someone else. Of course,

46

she wanted to clear her conscience by having a reliable witness that she had broken off her engagement to Oluf.

"So you think that everything is nicely settled and finished with, if only you write this, whether he knows about it or not?" I asked her.

"Haven't you read it?" she retorted. "It is finished. Now you have read it."

"But it is difficult for me to understand," I protested.

"I can believe that," she said, and walked towards the window.

"So you think," I said to myself, and I opened the cupboard.

"Don't you think it would do us both good to have a little drink now, my girl?"

"Please," she said, and sat down, smiling.

I poured out two glasses of my last good cognac. Margrete would certainly look askance if she came in and found us drinking, not that it would make much difference to my reputation in any case.

"Good health!" I said. "I don't want to hurt you, but I cannot begin to drink to anyone but Oluf."

"There is a lot of goodness in Oluf," she said, "but I have become something of a shrew to him."

"That's true," said I.

"I don't think he will be surprised," said she.

"But it surprises me, Annemari."

"You cannot make me believe that, Johannes," she said; "you realized it even before we did ourselves. You have tried to keep us together when really we were already apart. It's only because of you that this hasn't happened earlier."

"So it's my fault now!"

"I'm not jesting. It is your fault that I'm in this position."

"Another drink?" I asked.

47

"Thank you," she answered. "Tell me, Johannes, have you never wanted to do something wild? Something reckless?"

"No, of course not, never!"

"Is it true what they say about you and Rigmor at the Headlands?"

"If folk say it, obviously it must be true, Annemari."

"I don't know if I want it to be true, Johannes."

"No, you don't know," said I. "However, here's good luck to you, Annemari! It will soon be happier days for you!"

She put the glass down and exclaimed: "I don't like you any more. I certainly never expected that I should ever say that to you. But I have. If I thought more of you, I should throw this glass in your face, but I'm just tired of you!"

"I must remember to make a note of that in my notebook," I said; "it was an original retort. In the last twenty years I have sometimes thought of writing a book; now I have a few lines for it."

"Nonsense!" she flared. "I should think you have drawers full of your stupid writing! You merely pretend; you hide yourself, you middle-aged dreamer!"

"Dead center!" said I. "A bull's-eye! That shaft struck home! 'Middle-aged'—how true!"

"No, it isn't that," she said. "If you wince, it's never over something that hurts—you hide that."

"Yes, old foxes have old tricks!"

"I'm not blind," she said, "I can see you are better than him in many ways; but when I compare you, where is your courage—and your impulsiveness?"

"I guess it is Alexander you are talking about," I said, "and naturally I come a poor second there: that Aladdin has all the advantages! When the crane calls the wild goose, they both fly away!"

"Why do you keep calling him 'Alexander'? His name is Harry," she said, "but I wish . . ."

"What do you wish?"

"Nothing . . . but tell me what you are thinking! You just sit there and think that I have been with him, that I have been in bed with him! Don't you?"

"Naturally."

Annemari had almost shouted, never thinking about the woman in the kitchen. Did it matter? No doubt Margrete had stood and listened to everything.

"You mistrust me, I can see," she said, "and not for the first time, I know: you did when I was over in the town, too. You can depend on it, my friend, I have lived and enjoyed myself and loved whenever I wanted to!"

"Annemari," I said, "lift that book there, on the table. Gently."

"The necklace!" she said, no, she breathed it.

She took it in her hand and looked at it.

"It is beautiful!"

She ran the fine chain from one hand to the other. Then she laid it on the table where it had lain before, and covered it again with the little book, an old edition of Blicher's *Birds of Passage.*

There it remained.

We sat for a while. The clock gave a click—five minutes before the hour. "In five minutes you call the children together," I thought, "and you haven't found anything to surprise them today, and Margrete hasn't come in with the coffee but she can be excused, she is slow and she must eavesdrop."

"You don't believe me, Johannes?" asked Annemari.

"As a rule, my dear."

"It is finished now," she said, "you must understand that."

"Oluf doesn't know it yet," said I, "so I cannot understand it yet."

I was going to fill the glasses again, but there was no more cognac in the bottle. That annoyed me. I noticed that I was immediately a little hard on Annemari, a little extra hard, because of the empty bottle. I thought: "So Oluf's name is struck out in a chance moment, that is fine! You have got yourself a witness—it is grand!" I lit my pipe and leaned back. Annemari stayed until the clock struck. Neither of us spoke. They were very long minutes, like those before a parting. I sat thinking how often the two of them had come to this room, Oluf and she. I had practically married them. They had come separately—Oluf alone, Annemari alone. The wind blows over it, and it is no more.

III

SATURDAY afternoon. First I did a journey to North Greenland. Afterwards I visited both the Headlands and Kay's home.

> I often for a little solace
> Through my prison window peep,
> And send the while my sad thoughts winging
> Far and wide, with longing deep.

As far as I am concerned you need not take the verse too seriously, Nathanael. It just came into my mind as I went back into the schoolroom for the afternoon school. I had the dog sledge with me, and thought: "Now we'll go off on a journey!"

Yes, I found something to surprise the children. As I was going to the door to show Annemari out at the end of my dinner hour, I chanced to see the dog sledge standing on the shelf. A model of a dog sledge from Greenland. "That's it!" I thought. 'We'll go a journey in the dog sledge!' And in five minutes we were thousands of miles away from Sandö, up in Jack Frost's storehouse. Farewell Sandö and Annemari and all my troubles!

What do you think, Nathanael, are you any wiser for that long chat with Annemari? It was certainly a long, cosy chat we had with her this dinnertime. Yes, she got the necklace she wanted to borrow last night. "Beautiful!" she murmured. An ornament can whisper so sweetly to a woman. Then she put it down again, refused to take it. Yesterday she wanted it badly; today she doesn't want it. Isn't she a conundrum? Not really. When it came to the point, she was too proud to take it. But why so keen on it yesterday? Perhaps that is a bit of a puzzle. Otherwise, Annemari is no puzzle. Here I am with her letter to Oluf in my pocket. I am the postmaster on Sandö, my pocket is a temporary postbox, and I have to look after a little letter from Annemari, in which she breaks it off with her betrothed, Oluf. A sweet little receipt this letter is! And I had to read it. The parish clerk had to be witness to the signature, and be able to say: 'Yes, Annemari is free now, free as a snipe in the spring!" She can play with whomever she likes now. If she gets intoxicated by the spring with somebody else, she has a clear conscience. Annemari has been walking out with the engineer, while, a long way off, she has had a sweetheart called Oluf, who is little Tom's father, and perhaps Annemari has not been very happy about her position. There are some advanced-thinking folk who may judge that Annemari's behavior over this trifling matter was very old-fashioned, but Annemari could neither turn this way nor that without a little old-fashioned fuss in her conscience. Now she is free, with a brand-new freedom. It was cleverly done—just a stroke of the pen through Oluf's name. Now there is no one standing between her and the engineer. But their time is limited. The ice may break up tonight, or tomorrow, then the lover must leave. The two of them have, perhaps, only one night, a single night, but a spring night, and that is long, long, long!

I called the children in and took the dog sledge with me into the schoolroom.

Yes, in five minutes we were ten thousand miles away, away on a dog sledge!

Do you know the magic freedom there is in things, Nathanael? Not in thoughts, but in things, Nathanael, simple things like a dog sledge?

There are several ways in which one can try to free oneself. Annemari sets herself free in a trice, with a stroke of the pen, free for a new love that wells within her. Really, you know, she is still bound. She is bound by the bond of memory, and by a troublesome dream of happiness, a grand, false dream of love and happiness. Poor Annemari!

You can try to free yourself with great, clever thoughts, Nathanael, but I don't think it's any good. I once moved around under a dome of great ideas; I had a gnat-swarm of interesting thoughts hovering just above my head. But to what use? Had I anything I could say to the widow of a fisherman blown up by a mine? To what purpose all this everlasting thinking and worrying, when life is so fleeting and goes like wind through the grass? I couldn't think of a single word to say to Erik's widow, Lena.

So now I stick to the wisdom of nature and simple things, and the freedom they give as I stand and marvel over them. The hunter in the twilight, as the first migrating wild duck comes flying in, feels himself free, released, and uplifted. Or watch the rye-grass swaying in the wind, see only that, and you are free. Or take some soil in your hand, a handful of the timeless earth, a handful of peace. You are free, one precious instant.

Or take the dog sledge in your hand.

But we didn't begin with the dog sledge in the schoolroom. I put it on the display shelf above the blackboard. We wouldn't start our journey right away, but would prepare ourselves, on the quiet, by peeping up at the dog sledge.

"We will do sums first!" I said. "Take out your slates and arithmetic books." The cheerful clatter of slates began. The children sprinkled water on them from old perfume bottles, such is the fashion here, and dried them off with colored rags. The slate pencils screeched along the pencil cases, as they drew their lines. A boy came out to scratch his slate pencil against the cement base of the stove. Yes, we still use slates here. The parish council find it too expensive to use paper, and I like the slates really. On a slate, thank goodness, errors and failures can be rubbed out, instead of standing for an eternity!

So we do our sums. There is a vigorous mumbling of numbers and a rattle of pencils. There are twelve of them — seven girls and five boys. Only Kay is missing: he is lying at home with tuberculosis and must go to a sanatorium. The lightkeeper's children go to a better school over in the town. In our school there are only two classes, and they attend on alternate days, so there is a fair age range in the class and they don't all do the same work. After a while, one of them comes out to me for help with one of the sums. This is the way I like to do it, Nathanael. There is an art in it. I help them to creep gradually forward, until they themselves are suddenly aware of the solution to their difficulty.

But look! The sun is shining today! The sun has come home from its African journey. It stands adorned with long rays in its hair. There is frost only in the shade. The fields lie soaked, lakes of melting ice, with here and there an islet: smiling, shining tundra. Sallow ice still decks the endless surface of the sea, though it looks more soiled. The sea ice grows abscesses.

The sunlight floods, heavenly fresh, through the south windows, making a Milky Way of all the hovering motes of dust, and digging gold from the hair on the tops of the children's bowed heads. It sparkles in the stone in Inger's ring; the stone is glass, but it glitters like diamond.

In the sunlight, the painted roses bloom on the borders of the high wainscot, as they did to the inward eye of old Rasmus Sandbjerg when he was here and painted them.

It was two years after I came to Sandö that I asked Ras-

mus to paint the schoolroom. He was an old fogy that nobody bothered with, a widower, living alone in a dirty
hovel out towards the Sand Hills, but his door panels and
framework were painted bright with an old peasant art.
In a distant past, Rasmus had been the island's painter,
but he had been discarded when a newer, though poorer,
taste in art had come. He no longer had his brushes when
I asked him to paint the schoolroom, and the old man was
bewildered. Yet he came. He was here for months, and
the schoolroom began to smell a little of Rasmus.

He used to paint in school hours, too, and no one dared
disturb him in his work. He got paint splashes in his moldering beard, and took them with him when he died, they
were so firmly set. Yes, Rasmus Sandbjerg lies in his grave,
with paint spots in his beard.

He used to back slowly from the wall, his steel spectacles on his nose and his head askew, while he studied a
brush stroke in a leaf. No one dared interrupt him; once
he nearly fell over a desk and he swore an old-time oath,
but no one laughed. His inherited style was a commixture
of the elements of several styles, from Gothic to rococo and
classicism. He divided the wainscot into dark red squares
by ornamental foliage, with arches above, and gray, fluted
pillars in between. At the top, the pillars bore flower bas-
kets, from which foliage and rose trailers hung to the sides.
His masterpiece, however, is the door paneling, on which
he painted the Prophet Jonah under the palm tree outside
Nineveh. Jonah is in a frock coat and high hat. The palm
tree has three stylish leaves, but they are oak leaves. In the
distance can be seen the high church spires of Nineveh and
the Tower of Babel.

Sometimes the work would go wrong and he would become dejected. We were particularly careful not to upset
him then. He would sit himself down and listen to us at

our work, and then, sometimes, this old man, more than eighty years old, was assailed by memories, and would lift up his hand to answer some question.

Rasmus' schoolroom is the most interesting place we have on Sandö, after the church choir, and his rambling roses are the only things which connect the old art in the church with our present time. He wouldn't take anything for his work, but freely presented it to the unappreciative island, and when he had finished went home and died, full of days and contentment.

And now it is the last lesson of the day. "Come and sit here in the corner!" I said. We all sat on the floor in the corner of the schoolroom, with the dog sledge in the middle of us, and off we went—thousands of miles!

The sun makes the schoolroom sultry. There is a smell of smoldering peat, stuffed birds and dried marine animals from the museum over our heads—a hanging press of strange things found on land and sea—and a smell of rye bread, fat, and cold meat from the open mouths of the children. Their mouths are open, you know, because we are off on a long journey, and the mouth, as the doorway of the imagination, must stay open when the mind travels.

Annemari and all my troubles are forgotten. We are in North Greenland with Mylius Erichsen, Hagen, and Brönlund on their last journey in the ice-waste. Finally Brönlund is alone. His two comrades lie dead, left frozen to death a long way behind. He must go on, so that his body with the precious notes may be found.

> Never more alone was
> Soul upon a star,
> Facing death that lonely
> Night you stood afar.

His legs will carry him no farther, but the Greenlander, Jörgen Brönlund, still lies writing, with his frozen fingers, information for the polar explorers who, one day, will follow him. Yes, he does his duty, this lonely man, even while death overtakes him. Thöger Larsen says of him:

> Furthest icy wasteland's
> Frozen miles you scanned,
> Further see your dying
> Eyes and understand.

When I sent the children home, the fate of these men had so impressed them that they filed out quietly. Soon after, I heard them storming along the slushy road with wild shouts of joy. I, too, felt refreshed after the journey and the story of their brave, manly deaths.

I pulled on my rubber boots, slipped the dog sledge into my pocket, picked up my field glasses, and went out with Pigro. The dog gadded off over the field, however, and I didn't see him again until night, when he nearly frightened the life out of me. It is spring, and no doubt Pigro has enough of his own to think about.

My eyes were so delicate and sensitive after the long winter that the brand-new sun was all too blinding. The puddles in the shade, however, still crunched under my feet. Throughout the hundred steps or so to Grocer Höst's shop, I heard a lark. Favorite one! You who dare to waken thoughts of spring,

> And while the frost the sea's breast closes,
> Would open mine with songs of jubilation.

In the shop there were only the assistant and three cackling women. They gathered island gossip as their blue aprons gathered sunlight. The sun burst straight in through the shop window.

I gave my order for various things to the assistant, who, I saw clearly, was laughing up his sleeve as he copied out my list. I might just as well have ordered the two bottles quite openly, instead of writing out a list and trying to camouflage them with other things I had no use for. It will run like wildfire round the island: "The parish clerk is at it again! Four bottles this week!"

"Add it up," I said; "I will pay you now." He made out the account. I took the bill and looked at it. "You are wrong, my friend, it is a crown too much," I said.

I paid him and put the receipt in my pocket. The fellow was blushing, and all his pimples glowed scarlet. Serves him right! He should be more careful!

From my pocket I took another paper and pinned it up in the shop. In copybook writing it read: "As previously announced, there will be devotions, led by Schoolmaster Johannes Vig, in the church on Sunday morning at ten o'clock."

I put a similar notice on the door of the fire engine house. The island's village pond lay there, with sticks and stones in the ice: it stared like the glazed eye of Old Man Winter. The poster with the scantily clad woman, announcing the showing of the film *My Friend's Wife*, still hangs on the engine house door, where it has remained since the last visit of the traveling cinema. She has been frozen stiff, poor girl!

There, too, is the invitation to the spring ball at the Headlands. I hadn't intended visiting the Headlands, but found myself going that way as I swung into the avenue. The roadway was soaked and slushy with the coming of the sun. The Headlands lies a few hundred yards outside the little village, out towards the north coast. The farm is separated from the shore by a hill on which lie the black, thicket-grown rampart ruins of Old Headlands. West of the farm shelters the Fairy Glen, a grove rich in legend.

A car had recently been driven along the avenue, and as I walked I trod on the lovely pattern left in the roadway by the rubber tires. Frederik had been out in his new car that day. Naturally a man like Frederik, owner of the Headlands, must have a car, even though Sandö is only two miles long and doesn't possess a decent road. I walked in its track and thought:

"I hope she isn't alone when I get there! I don't know what I might do!"

I found a few violets below the willow hedge in the stack-yard. There is a certain air of greatness about the Headlands. It is, of course, the largest farm on the island, but it has an air of something much grander than that.

Perhaps it is its past, which here has simply turned to fragrance. On the hill towards the coast, the island kings, the kings of the Headlands, once lived, and to judge by the legends, now rapidly dying, they have not always had the best of reputations. One story tells of a certain Mistress Nitte, of whom, nowadays, little is known, except that she was not a good woman. "God deliver us from Mistress Nitte at the Headlands" is the refrain of an old ballad, which otherwise is forgotten. The red brick buildings of the dwelling are almost hidden among enormous elms and chestnut trees. In the farmhouse it is always shady with a cellar-like shade.

Frederik was at home. He and his men were busy tarring the whale boat, the well-boxes, and the heavy work carts in the large barn, where sunlight breaking through the slits between the wall planks made everything tiger-striped.

"Here comes the secretary!" called Frederik.

Frederik is an ambitious man. Not content with Sandö and the Headlands, he wants to get on, and he will, too! He is not a boss who stands with his hands in his pockets while his men work, he always works with them. He is a nimble fellow, slim and agile, a real snipe. He wears riding breeches and an old officer's jacket, though he has only been a corporal, but it becomes him. Spots and splashes only help to decorate the smart Frederik.

He proudly showed me how they had painted the boat and tarred the well-boxes and were now busy with the carts. I could see it for myself, but he had to explain it all to me. Everything had to be clear at the Headlands, everything had to be in order, and in everything the Headlands must lead.

I settled myself on one of the cart shafts and he sat down beside me.

"I had really hoped that you were not going to be at home," I said.

"Yes, what a pity it is for Rigmor!" he said; "she is longing for a little romance. Is there anything new?"

"Yes, the lark."

"And the starling!" said he. "But isn't it the taxpayers' register you want to look at?"

"Precisely!" I replied.

"I haven't finished it yet," he told me, and for the moment he looked flushed and self-conscious, something that only neglect of public business can do to an ambitious climber like Frederik. "It is spring now, and I have a frightful lot of work to do," he said. "You know I cannot run around watching for the birds like a certain parish clerk. But look in again on Monday! I'll slave over the register tomorrow, while you are providing spiritual food for the island."

"A man who lives as you do would derive a lot of good from coming to church," I retorted.

"What is the lesson for tomorrow?"

"The rich farmer who built his barns bigger."

"Enough!" said he. "Everyone says that Frederik at the Headlands is a prodigal who wastes his substance. Haven't you heard it?"

"That is exactly what the Higher Judgment would be," I said.

"Let us go in and see Rigmor, and have a cup of coffee," he suggested.

"Thanks all the same," I replied, "but I must go and see if the woodcock has arrived."

"Surely you don't think the woodcock is coming already, do you?" he asked.

"I don't know," I answered. "From woodcock and certain folks you can expect anything!"

"Have a drink, then?" he urged.

"Right!" said I, and in we went.

So we sat and had a drink in the Headlands' dark, spacious living room, surrounded by sham and ostentation. Rigmor stood behind me, smiling her twilight smile, no doubt, like part of the shade in the room.

Old Ole of the Headlands, Frederik's father, wouldn't have said "drink," but "dram." "Drink" is still a foreign word on Sandö, so Frederik of course uses it. He is a pioneer in agriculture, business, and society—and in debauchery and woman-hunting, too, they say, although only the evil or the most virtuous tongues say so.

That Frederik of the Headlands is ambitious and fond of company is true. It is also true that he mixes with a clique of younger people, not only from the island, who did well out of the war and have learned to entertain themselves in a gay, new fashion. Frederik and Rigmor don't lag behind in this, either. But, believe me, Frederik doesn't entertain without a motive. He is far-seeing and he aims high. He has his political dreams, and to be fair to him one must not suppose that he will abandon his great dreams for less worthy ambitions. The old humbugs on the island, who prophesy that Frederik will soon be wrecked, don't understand in the least what is taking place. Frederik aims high, is in many respects radical and progressive, and

61

wants to modernize. He has been chairman of the parish council on Sandö for several years, and during that time things have begun to take shape. I was secretary under his predecessor, too, and I can confidently say that Frederik is by far the more capable man. He is already the most powerful man in the islands out here, and he has influential friends and connections on the mainland. Yes, Frederik is certainly a high-flying snipe.

We are seated in the living room sipping cognac. Rigmor has filled the glasses but will not have any herself, neither will she be seated, but prefers to stand lingeringly and silently behind us, while Frederik does the talking.

As I sit here I find the cognac is having an effect upon me, so that, instead of listening to Frederik's chatter, I am wondering what her thoughts can be as she stands behind us. Frederik has been talking and only sipping at his glass, while I have hurriedly emptied mine twice. As soon as it was empty, her white hand came gliding past me to fill the glass again, and each time I have felt her shadowy warmth. "Who do they think they are?" I ask myself suddenly.

I have a strong impulse to get up, thump the table, and speak out, but I control myself, and let him go on cackling and flapping his wings.

To me this room seems gloomy and stuffy. Outside, the sun is still shining, but this big room at the Headlands is dark. Frederik has made a lot of changes at the Headlands since his father died, yet he hasn't dared touch the enormous trees, which stand so densely round the dwelling house that they shade even when leafless. Rigmor, like me, is a stranger on the island, but she is a woman of the shades who breathes the sad airs of the moon.

"To the devil with all these fairy tales!" I thought, and I drank up again. I noticed Frederik's quick side-glance and felt indignant. "They think I don't know when to stop! They think there's something wrong with Johannes Vig, now! Let them think! They should remember that there are some things I will not tolerate, and that, if I like, I can hold them in the hollow of my hand!" I boasted to myself. Yet I controlled myself. Her white hand glided past me again.

"Sheer ostentation! And sham, too!" I thought as I looked round the room, with its massive Renaissance furniture and the heavy gold frames surrounding the large, worthless paintings. Frederik has furnished it in keeping with his ambition, thus it is a picture of his own great plans.

"Here, madam," I said, interrupting Frederik, "I have plucked the year's first violets for you. They are for the Queen of the Headlands and for no one else!"

"That was deuced romantic, Rigmor," said Frederik, "and it came from the heart."

"Which had such wicked thoughts in it!" I said, and started to laugh, for I saw the jealous glint in his eye. Frederik is really broadminded, it is the modern fundamental law for him, but everything he is not completely master of makes him jealous.

"Thank you!" she whispered, and she held the three violets to her full, gray lips.

Yes, she is shade-like—gliding, silent, smiling—but only when she is seen behind the veils, of course. That was a silly gesture of mine.

Frederik, of course, has to retaliate, and says: "We are beaten men, Oluf, you, and I. That confounded engineer fellow is going to clear off with Annemari! How shall we get over it? I thought I, at least, had a chance, but these pier builders are the present-day heroes and women-charmers! Am I right, Rigmor?"

"Yes, my dear."

When I left, at last, I walked up to the Sand Hills to

cool my head a little. It was late afternoon. Cold blue clouds were filling the sky, and the sunlight was cold now. A slight breeze, hardly enough to stir the dead grass on the top of the gravel hills, blew in over the island from the sallow wilderness around it, and it was ice cold. The slush and mud thickened, then froze again. The ice lay as far as eye could see, but it had those dark spots.

"Like her," I thought; "she is lecherous."

The ice holes over to the northwest were chock-full of birds. I saw some whooper swans, and thought I saw a large flock of geese, but couldn't be certain. I had certainly drunk too much, and my eyes were streaming with water because of the wind, so that they wet the eyepieces of the field glasses.

I noticed that the dark spots in the sea ice now lay almost in streaks, giving it a speckled appearance, which reminded one of the wing of an immense bird of prey.

Perhaps she wasn't very experienced when Frederik brought her out to the island, and didn't know her own mind. In any case, she hasn't been able to tolerate the island, and this has become a kind of fever in her, a silent, dangerous fever, like the heat in a heap of damp, rotting leaves. She has, as it were, permeated the whole farm, so that to pluck a violet in the stackyard is to touch her.

I observed a little flock of oyster catchers down on the shore flats. Here already! They stood still on one leg and froze.

Walking down to the group of small houses at the foot of the hill, I turned in at the smallest and most dilapidated of them. The woman was taking the washing in from the line, two boys' shirts and some handkerchiefs, stiff as buckram with the frost. The line was strung across the little front garden, where the children and hens had worn away every growing thing, except the skeletons of one or two gooseberry bushes.

"It's good drying weather!" I shouted, loudly and boisterously. She looked at me half scared. Still young, but skinny and always timid.

"Has something happened, sir?" she asked quietly.

And I began to think: "Hansigne, here, is not a creature God allows to suffer from refined fears and hidden fevers of the mind. She is struck with His flail. She is placed, and places herself, where she gets flailed. I cannot for the life of me understand it!"

"Kay must go away," I said.

Hansigne turned away and took down the last handkerchief. A thin, maimed figure of a woman, she was now crying.

"They rang this morning," I said; "they have had a place for him for some weeks now. They will come for him as soon as the seaway is open."

Anders, the husband, came out of the outhouse with an axe in his hand. Stooping and gnarled to look at, he has the shifty, forbidding eye of a thief, but he's decent enough.

"Now, Anders," I said, "Kay must go away."

The very words struck Hansigne and she wept.

"Kay will be well looked after," I said.

"Yes, he will be well enough looked after," said Anders, and coughed.

"I believe that, too," said Hansigne, and turned her pale, wet face towards us. She went before me and opened the door. I stepped into the little bare room. The air was humid and saturated with the sweetish vapor of the sickbed. I had already taken the dog sledge from my pocket and was wondering how to begin. Kay must be told that he would soon have to leave for the sanatorium.

"He is asleep," whispered his mother.

His father had followed us in, and we stood quietly looking at the boy. I noticed that I was swaying quite a bit, and held my hand to my mouth so as not to contaminate the air, for I stood before the great purity of a real calamity.

Kay's brow shone like an anemone against the dark hangings. He had fallen asleep with a book in his arms, the book about Scandinavia's antiquity. We stood, all three, quite still and watched the sleeping boy.

IV

SATURDAY night.

I roamed about a lot during Saturday afternoon and early evening. I ran across this engineer I call "Alexander" but whom Annemari calls "Harry," but previous to that I went for a walk in the plantation, looking for woodcock.

> It was a Saturday evening
> I waited patiently;
> You promised me that you would come,
> But you came not to me.

Which reminds me, I visited Frederik and Rigmor at the Headlands first. I must talk about it, because I felt very indignant about it. I admit I had a little too much to drink at the Headlands, and gave three deathly blue violets to Rigmor, and ought not to have done so. Afterwards I said some wicked things about her, things I should never have said, some silly rubbish, Nathanael.

> It was a Saturday evening
> I walked and walked and walked.

I walked from the Headlands to that wretched house at the foot of the Sand Hills where Kay and his parents live. The lad took it calmly. I told him that he had to go away to the sanatorium. He took it more quietly than his parents, Hansigne and Anders, yet they had expected it for a long time.

I am an idiot! There never was much to spare in their home, and it's worse now. It has been difficult for a good many on the island while the ice has surrounded us, and

67

I knew it. If I hadn't been such an idiot I would have thought about taking something with me for them. Still, I had something—I had the dog sledge in my pocket.

They had nothing. Hansigne was obviously distressed that they weren't able to offer me anything, but she said nothing.

> But said nothing,
>   but said nothing;
> The parson made a speech
>   but said nothing.

So I invented that about the spruce trees—confound it! I couldn't think of anything else I could do.

I said to Kay's father: "It's a lucky thing for me that you haven't anything to do. I should like you to come up on Monday and fell those spruce trees in my garden; I want them cleared away."

"Those lovely big spruce trees!" exclaimed Anders. I was just as surprised myself!

"Yes, they will have to come down," I said. "I've been wanting it done for a long time now. They make too much shade."

He would be pleased to come and fell them.

There go my spruce trees! My lovely black spruce! Furthest from my mind was the thought that they should be felled, those dark, dense spruce, that shut out everything. My beautiful trees, gone up in smoke!

> You promised me that you would come,
> But you came not to me.

Kay was overjoyed with the dog sledge. I didn't want to give it away, because it had been given to me by a Greenlander I once knew. Yet here I go, boasting about giving it to the lad!

> I laid me down upon my bed
> And gave my sledge away.

Later in the afternoon I ran into the young engineer and had a long talk with him. He's a sociable young man and not without character. I can understand Annemari liking him, he is so sympathetic. I took the opportunity of having a dig at him, all the same.

I don't want to make myself out to be much better than I am, Nathanael. Not much better, but a little more interesting, perhaps. I have no ambition, my friend, but I'm not without vanity.

Try and see if you can discover this vanity, Nathanael. If you can't, it's your own fault!

Even if I have had too much to drink, I'm not fuddled. I can think clearly. I can feel that you've come closer, my strange friend. In a way, you're getting closer than I like. You would like to pry into my dark mind; you would like me to show you more of myself, be more open and frank with you, tell you everything, particularly what is disgusting and not so nice about myself. That's what you would like, isn't it? Keep away, my fine friend! Stand back, my friend!

> And every time I heard the door,
> I thought that it was you.
> Yes, every time I heard the door.

The oyster catcher is here. Half an hour before sunset, when the rays of the sun were long and as yellow as brass, I was walking along the low meadows, where the mounds of gravel push their way through the ice crust like toes through the hole in a stocking. And then I heard it: "Pli, pli, pli!" a dejected whistle. There they stood, a group of oyster catchers, freezing, standing on their thin, frozen legs, with their feathers bristling. Oyster catchers are foolhardy birds for daring to come so early. They are serious, purposeful, matter-of-fact birds, in spite of their red legs and long beaks—dandified, piebald sobersides! When I met the engineer a little later I thought: "If they call Annemari a snipe, then he is an oyster catcher!" A purposeful young man, with a pin in his tie.

I had walked on into the little plantation to look for woodcock. The little wood was perfectly still. It lies between the low meadows and the west cliffs, where it ends in wrinkled scrub—bushes that creep along the ground like tortoises. The trees in the wood are twisted and distorted: it is a labyrinth of thicket and stagnant pools. I missed Pigro. A good dog helps a man to see things he never would without it. I couldn't find a living thing, not even a blackbird or a chaffinch, no scent of a fox. The wood was dead.

And, of course, there were no woodcock. After a hard winter such as we've had this year, we can expect good flights of woodcock, but it's too early yet.

I turned southwards along the gravel road, towards the church and the little peninsula called The Hook. The western part of the island is the most lonely. There is only an isolated farm with two cottages, surrounded by deformed trees. Here the west winds reign. The Sand Hills, Western Hill, and the more southerly hill, on which the church stands, separate this rough landscape from the east of the island, where most of the islanders live.

Just before sunset, on the footpath leading to The Hook, I ran into the engineer. I suggested he went with me up to the church, where I had a little matter to attend to, so I said. He would like to; he had seen the church only from the outside: "A lovely Romanesque building," he said.

"A simple little house," I said, "but there is a funny

70

carved head in the chancel. Romanesque, too. You must see it!"

"I've been for a walk out to The Hook," he said; "it was off there that the little cutter struck the mine, wasn't it?"

"Yes, that is where Erik lost his life," I answered, "out towards the farthest reef, the Gysand."

"A peculiar name, Gysand?" he prompted.

"I imagine it comes from Gyge, the giantess," I replied. "There is a legend on the island that a giant woman filled her apron with sand from Western Hill and was going to bury Golö church under it. But her apron split and the sand ran out, forming the little islands, Birdholm and Gysand. The legend might mean that the island here was still pagan, while they had a church on Golö. Yes, our island is an old pagan island ruled by women. There's also the legend about the mighty Mistress Nitte of the Headlands, and there are others. But these are amateurish ideas, very homespun; nevertheless, there is a female power here on the island."

He took a side-glance at me, I noticed. His steps were shorter than mine, though he is fairly well built, yet he tried to keep in step with me. That is the kind of thing that one notices.

> For you have found another love
> And swept me from your mind.

I found this silly tune was back again, running through my mind. It irritated me.

"How is it you've never been inside? You will soon be going away, won't you?"

"Yes, it's to be hoped so," said he. "I hope the wind comes soon."

"It's not so much a matter of the wind coming," I said,

"as of its blowing from the southwest and the main current turning. Only then will the ice break. But I shouldn't wonder if it happened tonight. Try to keep awake tonight."

Tonight! I thought. Fancy me advising him about tonight!

"Yes, you should keep awake tonight!" I repeated, going farther ahead of him.

"I cannot bear islands," he said then. "I feel like a sick wolf!"

A sick wolf? thought I. A curious sight! I wonder if he has ever seen a sick wolf? An elegant expression!

"I cannot understand how you can stick living here, year in, year out," said he.

"When one lives here year in, year out, one sticks it out," I said; "but tell me, what is there at the end of it? What have you got out of it?"

The sick wolf looked at me out of the corner of his eye. I liked his mistrust. It was genuine.

"The chalk lime on the island here is well known," he answered; "it is of excellent quality, but if it is to be burned and used on a big scale, it will be necessary to build a new pier to ship it. The question is whether it will be a paying proposition, because a new pier will cost a lot of money these days. Naturally I haven't been able to complete all my investigations, but it will cost more than Frederik at the Headlands and the others reckoned on."

Now I can understand better why Frederik has taken a grudge against the engineer, I thought, though they were very thick at first.

"Frederik won't give in," I said; "there is nothing that will stop him. He'll make the island into a Klondike. There'll be a lot of changes here!"

"And you won't like that?"

"Won't I? I'll be delighted!"

72

"I had really expected to find it more old-fashioned here on the island, but it's pretty much the same as most places."

"Yes, perhaps."

"Of course, you know it better than I," said he.

> I got up on Sunday morning
> And began to comb my hair.

"Why should I know it better?" I asked. "You've been here for seven weeks, and I've only been here for seven years."

"Now you're joking!" he said, and he stepped out until he fell into step with me.

"No, I'm quite serious," I said; "I have found myself, by experience, that if a man stays seven weeks in a strange place, and has his eyes about him, he comes to know all that's worth knowing about the place. He can write a book about it, a good thick book! But if a man has been seven years in a place, he doesn't know the simplest thing about it!"

"Built of hewn stone!" he exclaimed as we were walking round the church. We had stood and seen how the lime-washed tower looked copper-red in the last rays of the sun.

It was very still beside the church, which lies high and isolated on the hill top. The air was icy cold and the gravel crunched under our feet. We carried on along the north side of the church, here and there brushing a hand over the cold, granular wall, whose plaster surface had been forcibly shifted by the hard stone underneath.

There, standing up against the church wall, was the propeller shaft, all that there was left of the blown-up cutter.

"That is Erik's shaft," I said; "it has got very rusted." There were old wreaths lying by its side, and a little bunch of fresh violets.

He walked on without speaking. I was glad.

> And began to comb my hair,
> And then to plait my hair.

"The church is built in a remarkably isolated spot," he said.

"The Headland kings first began to build it over by the Headlands, but every night someone pulled it down again, so they put a foundation stone on a cart, harnessed a pair of heifers to it, and allowed them to wander at will. They dragged the cart up here."

"A strange legend," said he.

"A common church legend," I said, "but the true explanation is probably that the hill here was used by the islanders as a place of refuge in times of trouble."

> I sat and combed me on the bed
> and combed my bed,
> I bedded me upon the bed
> and bedded my bed.

"Rubbish! Excuse me!" I said.

We went to the south side of the church. He could keep silent, an excellent quality, and there was nothing but what was good about him. With his long, well-shaped nose, and narrow, sloping brow, he is undoubtedly a man of character, but at the moment he is not sure of himself. In looks, apart from what God looks at, perhaps, he is a finer man than Oluf in market value. Of course, Oluf has his saga-like appearance and is better as a historical model. I often used to say to the schoolchildren: "If you want to know what Gunnar of Hlidarendi, or Olav Trygvason, looked like, just look at Oluf." Although this lethargic Oluf is only a sleepy Gunnar, I must confess, and he has been like this ever since Niels was drowned.

"Here lies Niels!" I said.

" 'Niels Jensen,' " he read, " 'was only twenty years old.' Who was he?" he asked.

74

"A gifted boy," I replied. "Niels was cleverer than Oluf, but not so bright as Annemari."

"Annemari is very quick-witted!" he said, and there was a lilt in his voice.

"Brilliant," I said. "Niels was quick too, but quiet; a dare-devil all the same. I was with them when they went to fetch Niels, after he had been found lying on the beach on Golö. He had been in the water thirty-seven days. It was towards the end of May and the sea was dead calm. The whole horizon was glimmering with the heat as we sailed home with Niels, or perhaps we were only dizzy in the head. At any rate, we were hardly real people as we ran in with him alongside the quay. There stood his girl, Gerda. Thanks be to God, his mother was not there!—she was already lying here. Robert shut the engine off, and we glided silently in towards the wharf. Then the smell from the boat wafted in towards them, as they stood waiting, and the girl laughed."

"She laughed?"

"Yes, she laughed."

"That was strange."

"Yes, but none of us who had been with Niels for two hours thought it was strange. Our minds were blank, although, naturally, we were afraid that Gerda might go out of her mind. We need not have worried, however, she is married now and has two children, and is happy. Notice how well the grave is kept where Niels and his parents lie. Gerda and her husband look after it. He is a fisherman, and they remember."

I walked over to the churchyard wall. "Come over here!" I called.

From the wall there was an uninterrupted view of the ice waste towards the south. It was turning blue under the cold, dying light.

"Can you see what looks like a dark spot out there, towards the southwest," I asked, "almost over to Golö? That is a large hole called the Bell Grave, where the current is often dangerous and there is an awkward eddy wind. It was there that Oluf and Niels capsized, in a very strong gale, in April. They went out in a sailing boat, arrogantly, for all I know, and Niels was lost in the Bell Grave. Can you see that long islet, way out to the southwest? That is Golö Reef. It's nearly three miles from the Bell Grave. That's where Oluf swam to!"

"Did he, by Jove!" he exclaimed.

It's as well for you to know that it's no wisp of straw you'll have in front of you when you come to meet Oluf, I thought, even if he is a dead lion now!

"It was two days later before we came to know that Oluf had saved himself," I continued, "for there is not one living on the reef. He sat there moping for two days, before some folks on their way to the islands spotted him, and we got to know about it on the radio."

"I remember reading about it," he said, "but I had no idea it was out here."

"Annemari hasn't told you about it?"

"No," he answered.

"Oluf will be remembered here, on Sandö, in a legend," I said; "one can almost say of him that he did as much as any man could do."

"I'm not sure that I understand that," he said as he jumped down.

I laughed and followed him, the solemn oyster catcher!

I unlocked the door and walked before him into the church. It was getting dark inside. In the narrow nave, with its low arches, it is always damp in winter.

"There was one thing surprised me," I said. We had stopped just inside the door, and I waited there to let the sound of my voice vibrate round the building. It always happens, particularly if one finds the tone that sets up a sympathetic vibration in the walls, even if one speaks softly.

"What was it that surprised you?" he asked.

"I was really surprised that little Tom grew into such a happy little soul. Annemari was expecting him when it happened."

"Hm," he murmured, and strode farther into the church.

No, you don't like that! I thought, even though you are a sympathetic fellow.

"Plain, but beautiful," he said; "are they the original Romanesque windows?"

"Only on the north side," I answered; "the Romanesque windows are narrow and high up, because they wanted dark churches, which are so much better for a feeling of devotion."

"Perhaps," said he; "in any case, I like the austere style."

"I had almost believed that men in your business had little time for the old trash," I said.

"Why not?" said he. "Many modern constructions are not very different from a building like this. But you were speaking about religious feeling. I don't understand how it is that people so often speak of religious feeling as if it were something everybody had. I don't know what it is."

"I think I said 'feeling of devotion' and not 'religious feeling,' but don't you think that the religious attitude is fairly widespread these days? People worship social doctrines as though they were revelations, and they worship political gods and technical gods and scientific gods and film gods."

"I've heard that it's part of your duties to hold services

77

here when the rector can't come," said he. "Tell me——
No, it's too personal."

"Go on! Ask it!"

"Are you a believer?" he asked.

"Yes, of course!" I answered.

"I see."

We stood without speaking for a while. It seemed to me, suddenly, that there was an urgent, driving pulse in the darkening church—dody—dody—dody—dody!

> I took me to the church here
>   but said nothing.
> I took me, I took me, I took me, I took me.

"You must see the head, before it gets too dark," I said. I had purposely waited until it was nearly dark. The gathering darkness was affecting him, otherwise he would never have asked that question. He did it to defend himself against something strange that was stealing in upon him in the half-light.

"You won't be able to see much of the Romanesque frescoes in the choir," I said; "they have suffered a good deal from the sea fog; but there is the head!"

It is a rough stone head that stands in the choir, turned to face the altar: chubby, like a seal's head, with round eye-holes and round mouth.

"Queer!" said he. "What is it?"

"Come here, closer to the altar rail. Look at it now."

"Death?" he suggested.

"Only the rector and the clerk see it," I said; "they see him there as the first and foremost in the congregation."

I could see that the stone head and the clammy, darkening atmosphere were acting strongly on the young man.

"I ought to run through one or two tunes for tomorrow," I said, "but it doesn't matter. Would you like to walk home with me? Perhaps you haven't had anything to eat, but I could easily find something or other?"

"Thank you," said he, "but I've promised to go to ... the lightkeeper's."

"Then would you care to come tomorrow afternoon?" I asked. "I think I have one or two things that would interest you."

"Thanks, I would like that," he answered.

I set a trap for him then by saying: "I haven't had a chance today to let them know at the shop, so will you tell Annemari that I can't come tomorrow for dinner?"

He said he would. It was easy! So she was going to the lightkeeper's, too, or neither of them was, but that they were going to meet was obvious!

He had walked to the door but stopped on the threshold.

"Can you tell me how it was possible? How he has been able to keep her here, year in, year out?" he asked impetuously.

"Who?" I asked. The fellow had temperament.

"It's a strange affair," he said as he stood there. I could just see his face like a pale medallion against the door. "That business about Annemari and Oluf, I mean. Her mother has talked about it. She is very open, Mrs. Höst."

"Yes," I agreed, "Mrs. Höst is very open."

"I can't understand it," he said.

"It's simple enough," I said; "it's over now."

"What do you mean?" he asked.

"You know what I mean," I answered; "Annemari has written and broken it off."

"Oh, that! Yes, I know that," he said. "I didn't mean that. I was thinking about all those years."

He lied! I could tell he knew nothing about it, but what did it matter? Did it make any difference?

"Excuse me," he said; "good night!" and he was gone,

gone with something to think about! Naturally it would look as if I had told him just as a matter of course, but I had meant it venomously. It would hurt his pride for him to think that somebody else knew that Annemari had finished with Oluf, and it was even worse for him, since he had known nothing about it. "Why should this confounded parish clerk know what I didn't know?" he thinks. The question consumes him; it burns and torments him as he goes to wherever it is he has to meet her.

But why did he not know?

I had no matches with me, and I couldn't find any behind the altar, where I often keep a box, so I had no light for the organ. I hadn't intended to practice the hymn tunes for Sunday, even though I couldn't count on Annemari's being at church to play. I hadn't even chosen the hymns yet, but thought I would play something for a while. I'm fond of the instrument. Like the frescoes in the choir, it has been spoilt by the sea fog, but it is a good piece of craftsmanship.

It is quite dark in the cold church now. I draw out the rumbling stops, and slowly begin to work the treadle of the bellows, until I feel that the organ stands poised like a huge animal ready to spring. The air filters finely through a leak, otherwise all is silent.

My hands fall on the keys. The howl of a storm spreads through the dark, empty church. I begin to weep.

Gradually the sentimental ditty, "It was on a Saturday evening," is driven from my mind by the pure mountain breeze of Johann Sebastian Bach.

I suddenly remember that there is a half bottle in a cupboard in the sacristy. I go in and find it in the dark, but I don't quite empty it—I've some sense of decency!

I grope my way back to the organ. There is a cold

draft blowing from somewhere, but I take off my coat. Now I will really play.

I play and play. Suddenly I stop. I go stiff with fright. Something has touched my leg and jumped up by the side of me.

"Pigro, you little devil!" I whisper.

The dog had had enough excitement for the day, and he had come, soiled and dirty, after me to the church, where he had found the door ajar.

I took another turn at the bottle, then sat myself in my stall, directly under the stone head. I clapped Pigro and patted his head. Brave friends! And I wept without shame, while the dog licked my hands.

V

O N Saturday night the ice broke. I was sitting in my room
when I heard it.

It was after eight o'clock when I rode home from church,
where I had sat playing in the dark. Yes, instead of walking, I suddenly had a horse and began riding home on its
back! I must have been out of my mind, or next to it,
Nathanael.

Perhaps you are wondering if I was ashamed of myself
for having laid hands on the bottle in the sacristy, or for
sitting in my stall in the church and crying like a child?
Don't ask! You must be content, my inquisitive friend,
that I have now shown a paltry weakness, shown myself to
be as unworthy as I am. I hope you are satisfied now, but
it isn't so often that I break down and cry. You can go to
the devil, Nathanael or whoever you are!

How did it happen? Do you think that I sat and whim-
pered because I was alone, or because I thought I was a
sinner, or because I had lost my plaything? Go to the devil!
I don't know how it happened. But remember, I had taken
a drop too much, and then a man hears great music when
he plays. God knows, Nathanael, I cannot really play, but
I know I can hear the great music, and when a man hears
that, he knows then that he is just a fleeting visitor here on
earth. Great music belongs to another world; it opens our
minds to another world; but just as we think we are coming very close to it, we find it utterly strange. We cannot
come near to it, cannot understand that world, and so we
cannot understand anything. Man is an immigrant in his
own birthplace, a passing guest in his own home, a fleet-

ing being on earth. No, Nathanael, the world you have a presentiment of, when you are full of a new sorrow, or when you are moved by great music, or when you are struck by the beauty of a verse, or when you see a miracle in the misty dawn, tells you that you are a stranger on this earth.

But don't take all this too seriously. I've had too much to drink, remember.

As I rode homewards, however, I felt strangely cheered, as if I was torn or split in two, but in a pleasant way, with my mind clean-washed and with a feeling of freshness.

I rode homewards, with Pigro skipping in front of me on the frozen road and the stars above me. Yes, I was riding, like a little boy at play, rocking on horseback. Here comes the parish clerk riding on a horse!

The moon wasn't up yet, and there was a slight frost. The frozen puddles broke to pieces under the horse's feet, then reflected the stars in my wake. Pigro was thirsty and stopped now and then to drink. It wasn't good for him, but I let him.

As the horse jerked and tugged at the bit, I thought the breath from his mouth smelt like mild ale, and I began to think about a banquet, with huge steaming hot dishes and tankards of foaming ale.

When I came near to Oluf's mother's house, I stopped and got off. Or the horse simply disappeared. A little way in front of me a light from the house shone into the front garden, on to the lilac bushes, standing with their branches stretched upwards like three-armed candlesticks.

I licked my finger and held it in the air. The wind was slight, but had turned westwards to southerly. The night was still, and Pigro and I stood quiet and listened. In spite of the frost, there was something delicate and living about the night, something that doesn't belong to a winter's night, a new diffused, scattered life. In the distance, the sound of a hen's cackle. I strained my ears, and wasn't sure that I really heard it, but thought I heard a distant quacking from the water holes, a swan's grunt, the cry of the long-tailed duck, and from the hills came a cry that could only belong to a lapwing. So the lapwing is here! A flight goes over, towards the east: "Gu, gu, gu!" Must be black scoters. They've been here some time, and now they move around restlessly.

Yesterday I pulled your leg, Nathanael. I told you that it was when the hunter stood among the rushes waiting for the flight of the wild duck that he felt himself freed and uplifted. That is nonsense. It is when he hears the piercing shriek of the duck flying over in the dark that he experiences something so utterly strange and incomprehensible; he feels a great sadness, like the sadness one feels when listening to great music.

I walked close by Oluf's mother's house, which lies quite alone in the hollow lane near the beach. Marie had lit the lamp but hadn't drawn the curtains. I would have liked to stand outside and watch her for a while, but she would have noticed me, though she didn't seem to have heard my footsteps on the frozen road. She has invited me to dinner tomorrow and I am very touched by it. Just for a second when I passed between the lilac bushes, I saw her large, gray head near the steady light of the hanging lamp. I didn't manage to see what it was she was doing, only her angular, gray head.

She is beautiful; hard, gray, and beautiful!

Living very much alone, she rarely talks to anyone and her quiet eye is almost feared.

Then, just as the elderly woman had disappeared from sight, it seemed to me that she was not alone, really. Although there was no one else to see, she seemed to be surrounded by people, not just a few, but great families. A whole tribe, or clan, of people was there in the little room.

On an evening like that one gets a desire to admire someone, to praise them, someone like Oluf's mother, Marie, someone who is alive on earth. She has a great influence on those to whom she belongs, and nothing can reconcile her to what she cannot like. I know that Marie came to the island from a much better home on the mainland, she came to be the wife of a fisherman in poor circumstances, yet she adapted herself to everything and has never been away from the island since for more than a day at a time. She toiled and became worn out by the island, as an old oar is worn and frayed by the thole-pin. Now she goes quietly and serenely through a decorous old age towards a befitting death. There is more of Sandö in her than there is in many who have lived here for generations. She stands here like a gray stone monument.

When I got home, I tried to read a little, but I don't know what books are coming to nowadays. The groceries had arrived from the shop, but I was disgusted with the two bottles of very poor wine.

So out I went again, leaving the tired Pigro behind in the room.

Though it is getting close to nine o'clock, there are lights in all the houses by the quayside, and the curtains are drawn as usual. Perhaps they are waiting for something tonight!

In the Ferry Inn there is light only in the little "den" as the men call it, which is cosier than the so-called "select" room. In the den, the floor is worn between the knots, and you can see on the bare tables the coarse red grain of the deal board. At the back stands the scratched black buffet, with its shining glasses, and the air in the room smells like juicy chewing tobacco.

Some men are seated at two of the tables, their caps down over their eyes, or the shiny peaks thrust up into their hair. They've had a little to drink, but their imagination has made the beer stronger, and they are feeling well disposed. It's a slack time for most of them as long as the ice lasts.

The oldest man present is the seventy-year-old fisherman Kristian, whose complexion has turned as pretty as marzipan through sitting indoors so long. Fat as an auk, he sits hunched up, peering out with his little sharp rat's eyes.

"The current is turning now!" he says to me. They nod round to me, their faces softened and mild.

"The sandpiper has arrived," says Valdemar.

"Oyster catcher," say I.

"The geese," says Peter.

"The spring herring won't be long," says Kristian.

"And the gray seal," adds Valdemar, who is often out on the watch.

They make room for me at their table, but I say: "I'm just going to have something to eat; isn't Elna here?"

"Elna is sitting reading a novel in the back," says Valdemar; "it's very sad, but she has grown tired of our faces, schoolmaster!"

"Who hasn't?"

They laugh. It doesn't take much to make them laugh tonight, for they have washed the thaw and the spring down into them with beer. Valdemar rubs the stubble on his chin and says: "We are sitting talking about a shooting-boat. Peter here has built himself one, without a soul knowing a thing about it. I went to see him today and found he'd made himself a shooting-boat as pretty as a sunset!"

"I don't want to boast," says Peter, "but I'm not afraid to say that it's a fine boat!"

86

"Does it gurgle at the bow?" I ask. "Does it not sway, and can you hang out over the side without it swinging? Or is it merely a trough and not a shooting-boat?"

"You should see it, schoolmaster," says Valdemar; "it is really well made and sits on the water like a miser on his money!"

"Are you joking?" says Peter. "You've never seen it on the water!"

"I can do that easily enough, without going to the water," says Valdemar; "it is an absolutely fine boat, Peter!"

"Sit down, sir!" invites Kristian, blinking. "What are you going to read tomorrow?"

"Look it up in the psalm-book! Third Sunday in Lent, first text for the day."

"Then it's the piece in Luke about the unclean spirit," says Kristian, and turns even more shiny in the face. "I can always remember it by the woodcock's coming the third Sunday in Lent."

"That's an old fable," say I; "others say the woodcock comes at Easter."

"It's right what I say," answers Kristian; "the woodcock always comes when Christ drives out the unclean spirit!"

"Then how is it we don't see it more often?"

"Because it hides," says Kristian; "but when Christ drives out the unclean spirit, then the woodcock comes."

Elna appeared. I ordered something to eat, and she went ahead of me into the other room to light the lamp, for tonight I would rather sit alone. It is one of the two depressing, select rooms, with yellow checked cloths on the tables, polish on the floor, and slight smell of mildew.

The light falls straight on to Elna's big, sour face, which is more sour than usual, and I say: "Come in and sit here for a while, Elna. You are not so busy."

"Why did I do that?" I ask myself; it was certainly not

87

done out of any spirit of helpfulness, but only from a wanderer's desire to study someone.

In a short while she came with my order and sat herself opposite to me. She is big and fair, with strong shoulders, and well over twenty. She went to school the first year I came to the island.

"Are you still satisfied with your job here?"

"Yes, I'm content," she answers.

I enjoy sitting here, without a thought in my head or having to worry about anything. I can hear them in the other room still talking about the shooting-boat and the woodcock. I hear Kristian say: "The schoolmaster won't believe me; he won't hear of it!"

"I don't think you are really content, Elna."

"No, I'm not."

"What's the matter, my girl?"

Why can't I keep my silly mouth shut? I'll land myself into a lot trouble if I don't take care!

"But it's no business of mine, Elna. I'm sorry I asked."

Perhaps that's the worst thing I could have said. She sits glowering down at my plate, without moving, but I can feel how she slowly swells up.

"I've been hoping that you would come soon," she says.

Uh! has she now? I go on eating, unconcerned, and I empty my tankard without looking at her. She can hold herself no longer. When they use that tone of voice, it is usually followed by a shower of tears, no gentle weeping.

"I'm going to have a baby."

"Really?"

"You knew I was!"

"No, I didn't, my girl."

"No, of course not; it was silly of me to say so. I only came out with it because I've had it so much on my mind, but I've never told a soul."

I start to fill my pipe, one of those pipes I had put on one side during the years when there was only poor tobacco to get.

"I've been sick. I wouldn't believe it was that, but it was, and I haven't had anyone I could tell."

I light my pipe, taking my time over it, because I must be careful what I am up to. She won't be able to stand my looking at her. She is like these loose layers of snow in the hills—just the waft of a bird's wing and the avalanche begins.

"It will be about the middle of October." she says.

"Hm, the middle of October."

"I haven't been like that," she says quietly, sibilantly.

"No, I know that."

"There have been a lot here who would like to, but I——"

"I know that, I know all about that, my girl."

I have to light my pipe again. I'm afraid I have let it lie too long without using it, because it seems strangely dead and is taking a lot of warming up.

"You can't help it if you are fond of somebody, can you?"

"No, you certainly can't, Elna."

"The others would have liked to ... but there was none of them that really cared for me, none of them!"

"I wouldn't say that, my girl."

"Oh, but I know! I'm not pretty and there's nothing about me. I've never been able to do as the others did, and now they'll all talk about me and point at me. 'Barmaid! What do you expect!'"

"Not those who know you, Elna. What about Annemari? She had little Tom. Yes, there was some talk for a time, but who talks about little Tom now?"

"Her!" she said, and drew herself up. "Her! Of course, you like Annemari, don't you?"

"Yes," I answered, "and why don't you?"

"Perhaps I do," she answered sulkily, but in her mind was a stream of hate towards the girl who was better looking and in a better position.

The outer door banged and someone came in, then he called from the other room.

"Yes, I'm coming!" she called, with affected correctness, but remained seated, and after a while said: "Can you understand that I've always thought this would happen to me, always?"

"Let us wait and see," I answered.

She raised her broad, sulky face and looked at me. It was blotchy and spotted, her tearful eyes all too clear, but there was something concealed in them, a little hidden sweetness perhaps, just a little. Elna is a sloe that must have frost.

"I have always known it," she says. Indeed she hasn't. Elna has certainly had a cheerless childhood, a mother she rarely saw because she was always out nursing old people. Elna is no ray of sunshine! She looks so sulky and heavy that she attracts nobody's sympathy and protection, yet Elna has had her dreams all the same, and carries the fruits of one within her. She thinks she has always believed she would have bad luck, because she has a catastrophe within her now. Her fate swells, fills the whole room, but I sit and hold it in check with cool, light, prudent words.

Elna is a real human being, on earth, I think to myself.

"The parish clerk won't believe it!" I hear Kristian say to the new arrival. It fills Kristian with a glorious will to argue, which warms him and releases his energies. "No, the parish clerk wouldn't believe the woodcock comes when Christ casts out the unclean spirit!"

They laugh and I can afford to laugh with them, since they are not laughing at me. I can do most of the things they can do, and although the parish clerk has his peculiarities and weaknesses, Kristian and the others with him think he is not so bad as a parish clerk. Of course, there are folks on Sandö who would rather have a schoolmaster of higher morals, and I can't say that they aren't right, but there are many others who take the parish clerk as they find him. With the thought, I begin to swell and grow, inch by inch, on my chair.

I sit and sustain Elna, binding her with easy words. There she sits, a heavy young lump, but a human being all the same. Now she is pregnant and something ungovernable is awakened in her. She will go straight into the sea if she gets the slightest push in the wrong direction, or she will throw herself at the first trampish fellow who will take her, because she is distressed and a great misfortune is upon her. It would take gigantic strength to hold her then, yet I sit and hold her with my little show of sympathy and understanding. I keep her here, but it is badly done. If I had any real human warmth in me, I would take her hand in mine and say: "Cry, my dear girl, cry."

"Drop in at the schoolhouse one day, Elna, if you would like to," I say instead.

"Yes, thank you."

More trouble and worry, I thought, as I stepped outside the inn and stood in the strange darkness of the night. The moon had just risen and was shining through the thick clouds. Elna hadn't said who the fellow was, so she had that to come and tell me.

By the quay, the ice-bound boats were tilted on their sides. The other cutters stood inland and towered up like leviathans and prehistoric monsters. The rough, shining ice covering the boxes and the wharf was loose. I threw some icicles into the harbor basin and they broke on the surface, the pieces tinkling as they flew in all directions.

There were lights in two of the rooms at the lightkeeper's, but the curtains were drawn. I could hear them laughing and talking inside, but I couldn't make out the voices. So you would like a certain necklace, Annemari? And why? Don't you shine enough without it? I think I'll give it to another girl, a certain girl at an inn. I think I might do that.

When I got home and had lit the fire in the stove I was no longer disgusted with the two bottles of wine and opened one of them. Pigro lay in his box, wagging his tail and looking up at me bashfully. The silly thing had been lying in my good chair as usual, and made a mess of it.

I looked up Sunday's text in the old psalm-book and read about the unclean spirit being driven out of the dumb man; about the house that is divided against itself and cannot stand; about the unclean spirit which, when driven out of a man, walketh through dry places seeking rest, and finding none returns to the house whence it came, and finding it empty, swept, and garnished, "then goeth he, and taketh with himself seven other spirits more wicked than himself, and they enter in and dwell there; and the last state of that man is worse than the first."

I looked across at the dog and said: "Yes, I can understand, Pigro, that the last is worse than the first, but I have no idea how it will go tomorrow."

After that I sat and cleaned my guns, and poor Pigro got all excited.

It was about one o'clock when I heard it first. From the sea came a long howl that rolled across the sky from one end to the other.

I sat quiet and could hear the wind in the spruce trees.

When I opened the window, the wind blew the curtain back into my face. At first I could hear nothing, but gradually I was sensible of a distant roar, as if it came from far below through vents in the ground.

As Pigro and I ran over the fields to the hill we saw the lights go on in several houses, but no one came out to the hill.

In the dim light of the moon I could see far out over the soiled ice field, but I couldn't see what was happening. It was quiet now and then: only the wind could be heard. Then it came again, and sounded as if a mighty flatfish was being skinned in the distance. Then an underground explosion and its thunder rumbled away towards Golö, and the roar of the water beyond. Then the cries of the birds flared up in the west.

There was another time when we stood up here on the hill and looked out to sea.

"He would not walk arm in arm," said Annemari. "Who?" "Oluf." That was a strange thing to say, I thought, and Oluf out there fighting for his life, or perhaps already gone to the bottom!

They went out in a sailing boat during a gale, Oluf and Niels, but why did they do it? Other young fellows have done the same. Why does youth throw its life to the four winds? It must be a tradition. They were out in the boat, before anyone could stop them, or tried to stop them. It wouldn't have taken much either, I think, as neither of them was a fool. If someone had said to Niels: "Listen, you! Gerda has begun to hem pillowcases!" it would have been sufficient; or if someone had said to Oluf: "Remember, Oluf, Annemari is going to have a baby!" he would have hesitated.

But no one said it; a myth called and they went out. Clever at handling a boat, both of them. Several of us stood watching them, as the boat rode on her leeward gunwale and they hung on the other. Farther and farther out they rode, over towards the Bell Grave. More came to watch, among them Erik, I remember, the dark little fellow who later was blown up by the mine.

Soon they were out of sight, but we continued to stare.

"No!" said Erik.

There was no more to say. I left the hill by one side, Erik by the other. When I got home I rang up the lighthouse; from there they could telegraph over to the mainland. Eventually I came to think of Annemari. On the way over to the shop I met someone who said that Erik and Robert and his two youngest sons had gone out in a boat, that Robert had forbidden his eldest son to go with them, so that one at least should be spared. This one had gone home and laid himself on his bed. He lay there gazing up at the ceiling.

Annemari at this time was going to have little Tom. There had been a good deal of regret about it at Annemari's home, a miserable regret, but not when Annemari was there; they were a little afraid of her, and she insisted upon having the child, at that time.

She was in the kitchen helping her mother. The old lady fussed helplessly around and seemed more upset than her daughter. Annemari seemed drawn in the face, otherwise there was nothing to see. She put on her coat, as it was April, cold and stormy, and we came out, the two of us. Mrs. Höst, her mother, followed us to the doorway, cackling and whimpering, and only when we were far enough away, and could no longer be seen by her mother, was there a change in Annemari; then she wept quietly and easily.

We walked on.

"He would not walk arm in arm," she said after a while. "Who?" "Oluf. He would never let me put my arms in his. He would only hold my hand as we walked, and that only when there was no one to see us."

She was walking by my side, with a firm hold on my arm. "He would not," she says. "Would," the past tense! Oluf is written off before we know anything! Then I begin to think about the little things that suggest something of the cynic in Annemari. For instance, that afternoon when she sat in my room knitting a vest for the baby, she held the vest up in front of her, then gripping it in her hand she said to me: "Johannes, this, here, will come between Oluf and its mother!"

Perhaps I misunderstand. In misfortune one clings to the little things, such as this, that Oluf would not walk arm in arm. It is perhaps the dearest thing about him, now.

We saw two women standing on the hill, a tall one and a plump one.

"No!" said Annemari, and stopped; we turned away from the path.

"I don't know, Johannes," she said, and hesitated. We looked towards the hill. It was blowing so hard that the two women stood leaning against the wind, their heavy skirts whipped by it. It was impossible for them to speak to each other, they stood too far apart. We could see the clouds and part of the dark sea between them.

Then we continued our way towards the hill. Annemari went up ahead of me, pushing her way through the raspberry bushes, that stood covered in young leaf-buds. The plump woman was Robert's wife, who put out her hand to Annemari and smiled quietly, but the other woman kept her back to us. It was Marie, Oluf's mother.

Karen, Robert's wife, said something we couldn't catch, it blew so hard, so we huddled close to her. "They are almost there," she shouted, and smiled.

I could see that they were only half-way there. At times the big boat almost disappeared between the great waves.

Oluf's mother looked over at me and nodded. She didn't

95

look at Annemari, but Annemari went over to her, put her arms round her, and kissed her on the cheek. Oluf's mother put her arms round the girl for a brief moment, then they separated.

It was a grim, chilling scene, and I had a presentiment that things would never be better after that, whether Oluf lived or not.

Bursting clouds rose over each other towards the east. The sea was speckled with breakers, which came hurrying in from the west. The sea is never so wild and strong as when it has just taken a human sacrifice. It was impossible for Oluf and Niels to have held out so long. We watched as the boat with the island's best men on board fought its way out.

As darkness came, Oluf's mother went home—alone. We stayed, and after a while we could see lamps and a swinging searchlight out at sea. A boat from the mainland, undoubtedly, but they soon gave up their search.

I stood and felt a strange sense of relief, while the sobbing girl leaned against me.

Is it really something I remember, or is it something I have invented, that I was with Oluf and Niels before they set out and yet said nothing to stop them?

Now I stood on the hill again, this Saturday night, and watched the dark fjord, stretching from the south through the ice towards the island, like a huge bird's beak.

VI

ON Sunday morning in church I read the lesson about the unclean spirits. There was a larger congregation than usual, due, perhaps, to their eagerness for the spring. The service was a short one, for hardly knowing what to say about the strange text, I decided to say nothing at all.

It is perhaps the best thing I have done for a long time, that I said nothing. What can I call myself? A Dilettante of the Faith? You probably know what I mean by that, Nathanael. Maybe a non-believer, who believes in what he does not believe. In a nutshell, I mean a Dilettante of the Faith.

Are you swept and garnished, Nathanael?

We two can't escape from each other. In any case, I cannot escape you! What I have to tell is for your ear only, Nathanael, and no one else's, but I will not be bound by your wishes. I always feel, somehow, you demand that I really disclose myself to you, covered with the clay I crawl in. You look for confessions that steam like hot entrails, I know, and you're very compelling, too, but don't come too close to me! Keep your distance!

Look outside! *The Barber of Seville!* A starling in the tree, right in the sun, so that the light shines on him. He sticks his rainbow breast out, swells, unfolds the feathers of his throat, and gives us an aria.

No! I decided not to say anything about the Sunday text. I was tempted, dangerously tempted, but what do you suppose I could really say about words like these: "As the unclean spirit driven out of a man walketh through dry places, seeking rest, and findeth none, then says he, I will return to the house from whence I came." What do you think of these words? Do you think that the parish clerk on Sandö can touch on so wild and strange an image? The unclean spirit, homeless and restless, driven out from his dwelling, a human being, wanders listlessly through waterless country, where there is nothing to drink, not even a dew drop, not even a blade of green grass. Have you ever thought of the evil spirit suffering, Nathanael?

Then the unhappy, unclean spirit thinks again of the home he has left and turns back to find it, and when he finds it empty, swept, and garnished, "then goeth he, and taketh with himself seven other spirits more wicked than himself, and they enter in and dwell there; and the last state of that man is worse than the first."

What ought I to have said about that, Nathanael? Of course, I could have lifted my chin, looked down my nose, and said: "Take care, my friends! This is a warning to those who think they are clean: those who have fought a strong and bitter fight, and feel themselves swept and garnished. Beware!"

But it would be only so much humbug compared with the text, where one almost feels the very ground to move.

With the ice beginning to break, I sat up most of the night, and consequently overslept on Sunday morning. I woke with a thick head, and felt so old: the bitter aching in my body warned me of approaching frailty. A drop out of the bottle helped, but there was no time for a morning walk to the shore.

Little strokes of bad luck, such as sleeping too long, are perhaps the worst. In my hurry I found Nanna's letter to Oluf, I mean the one in which she breaks off her engagement to him. It looked crumpled and soiled now, as if it were a generation old. "Take it easy and don't lose your sense of humor!" I said to myself. "What Nanna has written is no more important than if it had been written a generation ago, or a thousand years ago if it comes to that! Besides, it's no concern of yours."

Although I found it funny, I felt old and restless, and the letter caused me a host of speculations. Suppose the sea is open now, and the boat arrives today? Suppose Oluf comes today? What then?

It was an unlucky morning for me: I cut myself rather badly with the razor and I couldn't stop the cut from bleeding.

"It will be the death of you," I said to myself.

The blood was dropping on the floor, yet I was in high spirits while I went on with my shaving. It was a very wise thing they used to do in the old days, to bleed themselves; it relieves the spirit!

I stood and thought of death in a cheerful, elated mood. Why surround death with so much horror? It is restful: a man comes to belong to some place, he has no more troubles, and is free from responsibility. "I think highly of death," says Sigvat; "it is lasting and permanent. What is the world?"

As I stood in front of the shaving mirror, a truthful reflector, a chink in my memory opened. I was reminded of the forgotten thoughts of a distant age, when I was eighteen to twenty years old. At that age one can sometimes think calmly and profoundly about death. For many, the age of twenty is the finest age, for it is the age when we live most intensely. At twenty we demand purity; even though we tumble about in this and that and feel ourselves unclean, we still demand purity and truth. The more mature man understands nothing of this, he talks about his experience, the fool! His experience means only that he has forgotten, that he is utterly ignorant of the most important things. His wisdom means only that there are small deceits and lies, yes, lies, in all that he thinks and does. He has a good conscience, for he can no longer see that he is lying. He no longer sees life's great contradiction, which makes youth both happy and afflicted, ignorant and wise, at the same time. A young man is younger than a child and older than an old man. He knows nothing about anything, and all about everything. In an instant he is flung from the rich, blinding light of conviction into the darkness of confusion and dread; then he is flung back again. He is intimate with death.

"It will be the death of you!" I said to myself. My chin wouldn't stop bleeding. My handkerchief looked like the flag of Denmark.

Last night I read again Johannes Ewald's old tragedy, *The Death of Balder,* hence the pompous thoughts, Nathanael. The tragedy is an old one, and has the mark of age on it, but it made an impression on me, and that couldn't have been due entirely to the fact that I was tipsy, for I was clear enough to feel the force of Ewald's language. Surely there was youth in that bent old poet, Ewald: strong, enduring youth. Admittedly his pair of lovers, Nanna and Hother, are tedious, and the sympathetic warrior king is tiresome, but we still have a lot of men like him today.

Locking Pigro in the house, and with a plug of cotton wool on my chin, I set off briskly for the church. I took the lonely footpath round the north side of the plantation, for I wanted to be there in good time, so that I could think about the day's text.

On the way, I looked about me; the air was milder than it had been for a long time, several degrees above freezing point, but it still felt raw. Spring has its own peculiar way of being cold. I fancied myself walking and seeing with the eyes of a twenty-year-old. At first the light was too strong for me, for while there was a fine haze hanging over the island, there was a flood of light with it: a hazy spring day in which the sun wandered carelessly about, hidden behind a glaring veil. The plowed earth looked almost like a sponge, swollen and hideous, and in the ditches and along the grass verges lay mud and sludge and rubbish: ugliness! The hedges bristled with dark, tender stems, or floated out in slimy tufts like the hair of drowned women. Old Winter lay in aches and pains and bled to death in the shade. All that one saw, close at hand, was filthy and dirty, exposed by the shivering light. A solitary violet stood with a wan smile among the ugliness. The earth smelt of newly opened pits of rotten turnips. Thus it seemed to the imaginary twenty-year-old.

And what did the older man see? He listened first. He had already heard the sandpiper down on the shore, and the new note in the twitter of the chaffinch, which sat in the hazel bush and had already acquired the brighter colors in its feather dress. He saw, too, how the cold fields looked darker in the distance, and how shimmering blue the water pools were. The small ash and rowan on the edge of the wood looked as if they had just had their barks at the wash, and there were willow bushes which had turned red, red as red wine. The willows would soon have catkins, for I could see the buds were bursting to open, like a young girl newly entrusted with a secret.

It was a lovely day, and when I reached the top of the hill I got a shock. I saw that the sea was bare and living! In the north it was swept and clean, and out to the west the ice packs were moving northwards, but in the distance, towards the mainland, the ice still held. There would be no boats arriving today. That's a good thing!

Several cheerful titmice met me in the churchyard, otherwise it was deserted. Below in the distance, the beach

101

lay drinking water with ice-cold mouth. The ice edge was melting in its own water, and some crows stalked around and picked about in the seaweed, while an enormous gull, a great black-backed gull, lifted his beak towards the sun and sang.

There was still half an hour to the service when I put the numbers of the psalms on the board. I chose the first three set for the day.

I put the wine in its place in the sacristy, and then sat myself in my stall in front of the stone head, and speculated upon what I should say, but I got little inspiration. A stronger light was shining through the small windows now, but it only made the church look older and more gloomy. The nave with its low arches seemed more like a crypt, with its fusty, peeling walls and old reek of musty flowers. For the moment I got the impression that the church was a living, powerful creature, that it was the whale and I was Jonah.

I moved over to the organ and began to play through the music, but I had hardly played the first hymn tune when I heard someone come in. Someone I had not expected. Nanna, the March violet. Yes, it was Annemari, looking serious and a little uncertain. Over her dark hair she was wearing a red flowered head-square, which she untied.

"Here you are!" I said, and got up from the organ seat.

I sauntered out to the porch where the floor is covered with red clinkers. She began to play as I stood gazing out through the open door, out into the blaze of light. Some of the morning congregation had already arrived, but they were wandering round among the graves, as they usually do before coming into church. The gravel crunched under their feet, but otherwise there was a Sunday stillness. The people coming up the road blinked in the shining haze, and the light made their clothes look black.

She was dragging the tempo of the tune, which was not usually one of her faults. Then she stopped playing, came out into the porch, and stood behind me. I took no notice. There we stood.

"Why did you tell him about that letter to Oluf?" she challenged.

"If he shouldn't know about it, who should?" said I, "and how was I to know, Nanna, that he didn't already know about it?"

Then I realized that we had both stood there and neither of us had said a single word. I had only imagined we spoke.

"Why is it like this?" she asked.

And I replied: "The preacher says: 'God hath made man upright, but he has sought out many inventions.'"

I again realized that neither of us had said a word.

"Can you hear the lark?" she asked, and this time it was real, her voice came from behind me.

"Yes," I answered, as I moved outside and left her. I had seen Oluf's mother coming through the gate and I went forward to meet her.

"We can expect to see Oluf soon," I greeted her.

Oluf's mother looked hard at me and said: "You have blood on your face."

I thanked her awkwardly and went round the corner of the church to the little window in the sacristy, where I could see myself in the pane and wipe the blood off.

It took some time, my handkerchief became covered in red stains. Annemari was playing the organ again; then there was quietness and I heard the people go in.

I walked round to the north side of the church, not expecting to find anyone there then, but a few steps away I saw Lena, Erik's widow, standing with her three children round the rusty shaft from Erik's boat. Lena was bent down, putting the old wreaths straight, while the eldest girl stood holding a flowerpot with a flowering begonia, and the other two stood holding hands.

Turning back to where I had stood before, I heard the sound of a car crawling up the hill. It must be Frederik from the Headlands, so I would wait a little longer, although the bleeding had stopped.

After a while, I heard Lena and the children walking slowly towards the corner. I had to move away, so I walked round to the church door, and there I ran into Rigmor.

She had left the car in the road, and was walking up the path from the gate. Pretty—devil take her!—in a gray spring costume that fits her like a glove.

"You haven't brought your pious husband with you, dear Rigmor," I said, taking her gloved hand, a hand with amorous intentions, delicate but audacious.

"Sorry to disappoint you," she said. "Frederik has to stay at home and do some work on the taxpayers' register."

Erik's widow and the children walk slowly past. They have been looking at an idol, a rusty propeller shaft. They greet us very gravely and humbly, as if they were walking on a forbidden path, which vexes me, for there's no reason why they should almost creep past her and me: they possess something we don't. We stand and watch them carefully scrape their boots on the iron scraper and then, one after the other, wipe their feet on the mat before they go in. The humble and meek of the earth.

"Well, Rigmor," I asked, "are you swept and garnished?"

"I suppose that's one of your jokes?"

"My dear, you are bored at home, aren't you? Frederik ought not to take on so much work."

"My dear," she said, mimicking the tone I had used,

and laughing, cooing like a dove. "I'm never bored when Frederik is busy. But why do we see so little of you?"

"I should like to come oftener, but when can I find you at home? You are always in company."

"I'm tired of that crowd," she says. She says it with her little infectious smile, which infects me, not with smiles, but with certain other thoughts. So she is tired of Frederik's clique. She can't demoralize them; they are already demoralized.

"They cannot romanticize, Johannes," she added, laughing again in her gentle way.

Romanticize! What does she mean by that? Isn't that what they say about certain amorous dances? I can easily imagine what she might mean by this veiled word—all that is secret and hidden in the recesses of a house, the recesses of words, the recesses of the body. Romanticize! I should never have given her the three violets, for without them she would never have come today. Devil take her! But you can never tell with Rigmor; she is double-tongued.

"You underestimate them," I said. "There is that manly Alexander, the engineer, isn't he entertaining?"

"In a way," she replied, so sweetly that I could chop her up into malt sweets, but so preoccupied, so preoccupied.

"You must get away from the island, Rigmor. We must push Frederik on, so that he becomes president or minister for something, then you'll get away from this molehill."

"I love the island," she said; "but come home with me to dinner?"

"Thank you," I replied, "but I've promised to go to Oluf's mother for my dinner today."

"Will you enjoy that?"

"Immensely! I've almost invited myself. An old woman and a cold one, too; it should be nicely free from excitement."

"You have a lot of duties, Johannes. You should come with me, all the same. Marie is a grand woman, but can't you go there another day?"

"Off with you!" I exclaimed. "Now you can all go to blazes!"

She smiles with her full, gray lips, and goes before me into the church. One would hardly call her beautiful, she is almost too plain and noble, almost colorless, until one is sensible of this atmosphere there is about her.

Annemari turned and saw us. The two women nodded and smiled sweetly to each other, then Rigmor walked to one of the rear pews. Previously the Headlands had used the front carved pew, but nowadays it was finer to sit in a more reserved position at the back.

I walk up to my stall, where I can sit almost hidden from the congregation. I sit and wait, as there are still some minutes before the service begins. I haven't had much chance to think about the day's text, but I have an idea that it won't be too difficult to find something to say.

I have the stone head almost right in front of me, everlastingly glaring at me with its round eyes. I saw him like this, early one morning in a winter fog, in the gray light just before daybreak, when I was lying in the shooting-boat over by Brundholm. I had intended to land on the island to wait for the geese coming in, but the fog thickened and I lay where I was in the boat. The water was like oil, and the sound of the drops dripping from the wet oars seemed almost too loud. There wasn't another sound. Then, suddenly, he stood there in the water, right beside me, with the same round head and glazed eyes! We looked each other in the eye for a short while; then he was gone, leaving only the desolate water and the desolate fog.

It was a seal, of course, just a spotted seal. I have often seen them, have even hit several of them, and then fished after them with a hook as they lay on the bottom. We often hear their hooting. Nevertheless, one still has the idea that perhaps he will come again, but in another guise.

However, I have no serious thoughts about death as I sit here this morning, facing the stone head. I have no serious thoughts at all, only light, trivial, fickle ones.

No, there is nothing serious about me, in the last few minutes before I step forward to read the old opening prayer. The bell is not ringing today. It rings only when the rector is here, so I shall decide myself when it is time to start the service. These last few minutes are often long, worrying, and unmanageable, for so many light, rustling ideas sweep through my mind.

They are waiting and I wait. Their expectation is becoming something that I can almost feel with my fingers, a tangible substance, yet here I sit in my stall and get silly ideas. I wonder what would happen if I stuck a big black beard on my chin and then stood up with it on. Or if I suddenly started to crow like a cock? Yes, a little frivolous devil with his tricks has got hold of me, and I sit here and turn into a market clown!

They still wait, and as each second passes I can feel more and more strongly, and today more clearly than ever before, the hostile force that steals towards me from the congregation gathered in the church, as if a giant were slowly approaching me, with his hands half open, his gaze directed towards my windpipe. In the instant that I rise I shall come to grips with him, I know.

I remain seated. The expectation thickens.

This indefinable, hostile force, which would grip me by the throat, does not emanate from certain opponents I have among the churchgoers, folk who do not find me worthy of my calling; it arises from my duties as parish

107

clerk on the island. Not one of them out there has any idea what a strangling power they have sent against me. It has developed against me in these few moments during which their anxious waiting has united them into one fellowship, outside of which I stand alone.

They are not yet a congregation, Nathanael, for a congregation is perhaps like great music, or like the miracle of dawn, supernatural and incomprehensible; but as their expectation almost physically tightens its hold on them, their minds are tuned in the same direction. Were I a true and humble servant it could perhaps become an inspiration, whereas I feel it as a powerful hostility. Who am I who sit here? A stranger, a guest of the moment, a chance stranger on the earth, though in a short while I shall stand up and be their voice.

There are between thirty and forty of them in the church—more than usual. Some of them are more doubters than believers, hardly knowing what to think about the confusion of the present day. For some of the others, belief in God is perhaps a thin Sunday habit; but there are some for whom God's Word is as real as the soil in the field or the salt in the sea. Such it is for the quiet Robert and the talkative Kristian; for them everything here is just as real as the hooks on a night-line, set in the sea. Now, in the stillness, these souls sit and become the kernel of a fellowship which slowly consolidates. They are my potent enemies.

In the final seconds I glance around me and see the half-obliterated Romanesque fresco paintings. I wonder if there is anyone else in the church who understands the beauty of the place as well as I do, or who is so intimate with its history? No, of course not! Yet I am the stranger here, the ephemera. It is they out there who really own the place, I feel. And now this mysterious union is about to take place, but perhaps it is only mysterious to me, the stranger, and to the others simple and plain sailing; and then I realize that the church is something else besides an historic building. It has its strong, inexplicable existence in the present. Yes, a strange existence, without age, for they who now wait in the nave have been here since the church was consecrated, and will be here as long as it stands, I think to myself.

"Now!" I say to myself. I half rise and then sit again. All the whispering between the pews has stopped. The air is charged. The silence tightens with immense power round each and all.

Their expectation, a superior enemy, opposes me. There's nothing I can do, think I, except be honest, empty, and light, as I am. Am I not swept and cleaned? I am emptiness, nothing.

All at once I am aware that I have got up and have stepped forward under the broad choir arch. I discover that I'm standing here, looking calmly down over them. I see their faces and yet I don't, meet all their eyes and yet meet none.

It's as if my real self, my own will, has been left behind, still sitting in the stall, and only now my real self gets up and walks towards the body, the soul's frame, which stands under the choir arch; but no union takes place and I continue to have the feeling of being split, of being twofold. I stand in dead and idle stillness and look down at their faces for deep, painful seconds. A misgiving glides, cold as an eel, into my consciousness, but doesn't disturb my peace. You are possessed! A stranger, a more powerful stranger, filled your emptiness as you rose. You are possessed! It is an evil spirit that stands here now. They are the evil spirit's eyes that hold their eyes fast now. It is a fiendish delusion!

If someone came to me and wanted to debate the existence of the Devil, I should make light of it.

Perhaps it is the arrogance of emptiness, the pride of

nothingness in me, which, coming unexpected, has broken out as power: I don't know. But it's as though a powerful and cunning spirit dwells within me, and makes me feel more strongly masculine. His mouth is curled in a soft, seductive smile, and the congregation no longer have wills of their own. The women are bewitched. Annemari sits powerless at the organ.

All their faces are round, flabby, and stupid. Robert sits there with his crocus-blue cheeks and white brow, round and stupid, and old Kristian is hypnotized like a hen. What was it you said, Kristian, about the woodcock coming when Christ drives out the unclean spirit? The time has come, let us see if the woodcock comes, you superstitious old fool! And there sit Hansigne and Anders, Kay's mother and father, round and stupid: they've forgotten all about Kay. There sits Gerda, round and stupid, the young Gerda, Niels's sweetheart before he was drowned, but she's happy again now. But who is that beside her? Sitting next to Gerda is a big, coal-black face without eyes. It was terrifying for the moment, till I saw that it was only a woman with her head bent forward; her round felt hat looked like a face. It is Lena, Erik's widow, the only one who is not gazing up at me, the only one perhaps who isn't captured. Look this way, Lena! You must not hide yourself, we must be united and one!

I am gratified by what I see. It is not the gratification of goodness, but I am satisfied that I have reduced them all to souls in an underworld, from which only their heads emerge. Now they're all like the head that rose out of the water and the head in the choir—all dead bodies.

"Lord, I am entered into this Thy House to hear what Thou, my God and Creator, shalt say unto me . . . ."

"Amen."

The stranger is not ousted by the prayer, nor does he

stumble over the words. But in the pews, below, there is a slight relaxing, which shows itself as the faces become firmer and begin to acquire their usual expressions of glumness or slyness, harshness or kindness, though not completely, for they are still bound by the strange power.

I nod to the puppet at the organ and she begins to tread the squeaking bellows. The gathering of specters begins to sing, "A safe stronghold our God is still." I lead the singing, one hand resting on the front pew, where the paint is worn away and the wood polished by the hands of previous parish clerks. At other times I find it a help, I feel linked with the many clerks, the many poor, empty hearts, who in the past have stood here and made it holy; but today it cannot budge the grip of the stranger, he is in charge.

I read the Epistle in which Paul warns the congregation in Ephesus against fornication, all uncleanliness, converse with the wicked, and foolish talk. For me and for him who stands within me they are empty words, but he tries to make his voice musical to preserve the spell.

We sing the next hymn, "Then shall Satan's kingdom be cast down," and the stranger smiles cunningly.

If it is myself he would bedevil and corrupt, it is hardly necessary, but I am become a tool to bewitch the others. It is their trust and faith he would contaminate, their Christian faith he would execrate.

They continue to sing. In the second pew stands Lena, Erik's widow, with the children on one side of her, the boy on the outside as a little protector, and on the other side Gerda, happy again. It was Erik who went out to help Niels, and Gerda has not forgotten it, she always sits next to Lena. She has gone to Lena's a lot since Erik was lost, but what can the red-cheeked Gerda say to the widow? Nothing much, nothing worth hearing.

Lena is dressed up, I see. Her hat is hardly new, but

111

someone who is handy at that kind of thing, Gerda perhaps, has given it a new style. She has got herself a new black coat, or had her old one turned, and she looks nice in it. One must look nice when one is in mourning, for those in grief are the object of other people's attention, and one can see that Lena has taken care over her appearance. The children, too, are nicely dressed. I should think Lena has had a busy time this morning, rushing about getting them ready. What has she got to keep them on? Nothing much. There won't be much left of the compensation for the loss of the boat, since Erik owed most of it, but one has to be dressed, one must look nice.

The boy shares a hymn book with his sisters. He reads a line, looks up from the book, and stares out of the south window, into the sun's haze, while he sings it. He reads the next line, and looks out of the window again; looks down, looks out. He is dark like his father, needs to have his hair cut and his nose wiped. Looks down and reads, looks out and sings; looks down, looks out. Is there any meaning in it for him? Is he thinking about his father now and finding an explanation that eludes me? Surely not. It's fantastic to think that a little fellow like him can understand something I cannot. He just looks unthinkingly at the lines, thinks nothing, knows nothing, looks down and reads, looks up and sings, and knows nothing of what he is doing.

The stranger who stands here leading the singing directs his malice first and foremost at the little dressed-up group, the widow and her children.

In the Gospel according to St. Luke it is written:

"And he was casting out a devil, and it was dumb. And it came to pass, when the devil was gone out, the dumb spake; and the people wondered. But some of them said, He casteth out devils through Beelzebub the chief of the

112

devils. And others tempting him, sought of him a sign from heaven. But he, knowing their thoughts, said unto them, Every kingdom divided against itself is brought to desolation; and a house divided against a house falleth. If Satan also be divided against himself, how shall his kingdom stand? because ye say that I cast out devils through Beelzebub. And if I by Beelzebub cast out devils, by whom do your sons cast them out? therefore shall they be your judges. But if I with the finger of God cast out devils, no doubt the kingdom of God is come upon you. When a strong man armed keepeth his palace, his goods are in peace: but when a stronger than he shall come upon him, and overcome him, he taketh from him all his armor wherein he trusted, and divideth his spoils. He that is not with me is against me; and he that gathereth not with me scattereth. When the unclean spirit is gone out of a man, he walketh through dry places, seeking rest; and finding none, he saith, I will return unto my house whence I came out. And when he cometh, he findeth it swept and garnished. Then goeth he, and taketh to him seven other spirits more wicked than himself; and they enter in and dwell there: and the last state of that man is worse than the first. And it came to pass, as he spake these things, a certain woman of the company lifted up her voice, and said unto him, Blessed is the womb that bare thee, and the paps which thou hast sucked. But he said, Yea rather, blessed are they that hear the word of God, and keep it. Amen."

They settle down. The wave subsides, but moves violently under the surface. I feel a strong temptation. They see this strange text before them as a hazy, foggy landscape; and HE would have me bewilder them further with poetic descriptions.

The text is difficult and awesome and I have broken out

in a sweat. I notice Erik's boy, with the long hair, sitting poking his nose, while he looks towards the window and gazes out with a far-away look.

"Lena!" I hear myself say. "Now you must understand. Has the Son of God helped you?"

The widow looks up, looks past me, looks at something behind me with wide open eyes! She nods.

I thought someone walked past me, and felt a blow that rocked me on my feet.

After we had sung the last hymn Annemari got up and went quickly out.

I walked back into the choir, stroked my hand over the stone head, and went into the sacristy, closing the door after me. I sat down on the chair and nearly overbalanced, it was so old and loose in the legs.

You must give up this tippling, I said to myself. At intervals I had a buzzing in my ears, as if I had had a slap in the face, but when I became really aware of this sound, I recognized it. It was the rumble the woodcock makes when it takes to the air.

VII

TOWARDS midday on Sunday, I was sitting in the room at Oluf's mother's house, looking through a photograph album, and was reminded of the time when Oluf was not allowed to speak out about the terrible thing that had happened to him.

But before that I had sat alone for a while in the sacristy, after that experience I had in the church. What do you think about it, Nathanael? It must have interested you, and you would like to know more about it. Well, I have confessed that I felt myself possessed of the Devil during the service. Nothing less! Weren't you delighted over that confession, that I, who was neither one thing nor another, but only inward emptiness, suddenly became the seducer himself? I felt like a stranger at the meeting, and then became so completely a stranger that I was like the Devil himself. Weren't you in ecstasies over it, Nathanael? Or don't you believe a word of it? What do I believe myself? Perhaps you say the same as I said to myself in the sacristy: I must be crazy to drink in the morning, on an empty stomach. Isn't that right?

I shan't trouble you with the thoughts that passed through my mind as I sat on the ramshackle old chair in the sacristy. At first I sat watching the shadows rotate across the whitewashed ceiling, as the people passed the little window on their way from church. Then everything went quiet. I missed Pigro. The sacristy is a melancholy little room. In one corner stands an old deal cupboard, warped by dampness, and in another a hand basin, above which hang a tarnished mirror and a towel.

When I left, I had intended to go for a walk along the beach as far as The Hook, though I knew I hadn't time to get there before I was due at Oluf's mother's for dinner, but when I came out of church and had locked up after me, I saw the car from the Headlands standing outside the gate. Rigmor was sitting waiting in it, and she lowered the window. "Ugh!" she exclaimed, and shuddered. I noticed that she didn't look at me.

"Get in!" she said.

I got in and sat at the back.

"There's plenty of time before dinner," she said, without turning; "shall we run out to the cliff and look at the sea? You could tell me about the birds."

"No, we won't!" I answered.

"I'll bring you back to Marie's," she said, taking out a cigarette and handing the packet to me over her shoulder.

"Shall we?" she asked again; "I should like to hear you tell me something ... about the birds. Just for half an hour."

I laughed, but gave her no answer. So Rigmor had been affected, and perhaps had waited here because she was a little afraid of what I might do when I was left alone in the church!

"Shall we?" she asked.

A long way below in the hills I could see a figure, quite small; it was Oluf's mother on her way home.

"Johannes, that was strange in the church."

"Get started!" I said.

She started. I met her gaze in the little mirror over the windshield, but she immediately withdrew.

"Let me out when we reach Marie," I said.

She drove hard over the slushy, pot-holed road, the splashes from the wheels obscuring the shining landscape. Rigmor pulled up as we reached Marie, opened the door, and called: "Get in, I will run you both to your house!"

I should never have thought that Oluf's mother would accept, but she got in beside me, and we drove on.

"This is my first ride," said Marie, "I've never been in a car before."

She sat erect on the seat and bobbed up and down. Her smile and the bobbing were not quite like her, I thought.

"I must take you for a drive one day, Marie," said Rigmor; "some day when we have to go over to the mainland, you must come with us. But who is that down the road?"

Rigmor knew all right: it was Annemari walking quickly ahead.

"Let us see if she will come," said Rigmor.

I didn't expect Annemari to accept, but she got in the front beside Rigmor. How delightful!

"You are coming to the spring ball tonight?" said Rigmor to Annemari.

"Thank you very much indeed," said Annemari.

"That's fine!" said Rigmor, "but I mean Harry, too; he will come, won't he?"

"He would like to very much indeed," answered Annemari.

"Good!" said Rigmor. "Marie, aren't you coming to the spring ball?"

"Thank you," answered Oluf's mother, "but it is so long since I went anywhere."

She sat bolt upright and bobbed about, and the color had come to her cheeks. I didn't like it.

"Then come!" said Rigmor. "And are you coming, schoolmaster? You owe me a lot of dances!"

"Poor schoolmaster!" said Annemari; "he has so awfully much to do, and he says he's getting too old, but just you invite some young folk, Rigmor, and he'll be there!"

It seemed to me the two women were a little hectic and false. Moreover, Annemari was being venomous, here, towards Rigmor, who was thirteen years older than she.

We had stopped in front of Marie's house.

117

"Whom would you suggest, then, Annemari?" asked Rigmor.

"If I may be allowed a suggestion," said I, "I propose you invite Elna, the barmaid. I like her very much."

"That was glorious!" exclaimed Rigmor.

"The schoolmaster is always so awfully frank," said Annemari.

"Frightfully earnest!" said Rigmor; "a Samaritan, that's what he is!"

"Yes, so soft-hearted," said Annemari.

"But why don't you say something?" asked Rigmor.

"Horses, dogs, and men can be tamed, but cows, sows, and women, there's nothing you can do about them," I said; "but if you turn round and look across the meadow you can watch a little drama."

Over by the marl-pit in the meadows, two large hares were fighting, while another pair sat watching them excitedly close by. One of them, a broadheaded male, now made a rush at the two that were fighting and whirled round with them. Then out he sprang and back he came to the doe, who sat enjoying it all. Presently he began to flirt with her, and she surrendered, while the two other males fought like mad, tumbling about and flaying each other, hair flying in all directions.

Rigmor laughed and glanced up into the mirror, but Annemari had turned away and was looking at her watch.

"Have you ever picked up a piece of fur from a hare," I asked, "while it's still warm and spotted with blood, and held it to your nose and smelt it? It is wild!"

"Wild!" I repeated, for I recalled it strongly.

When Marie and I got out of the car, I said: "I've just remembered something, Rigmor. Young Kay ought to have been away to a sanatorium long ago, and there's a place ready for him now. He should go as soon as possible,

118

but it will delay matters if we have to wait until they come across for him. It has just struck me that Frederik or you may be able to take him in the car?"

"Gladly," she answered, and looked at me.

You have a suspicion, thought I, that I just hit upon this to test you, for there are some who daren't go near the house where Kay is.

"Only to the boat," I added, "we can arrange for transport from the harbor."

"Perhaps we could take him all the way to the sanatorium," said Rigmor. "Frederik has to go over as soon as he can and we would do it gladly."

"It's frightfully good of you!"

I stood leaning against the kitchen door in Marie's little house, smoking my pipe, while she began preparing the dinner. With a large starched apron over her heavy, dark gray dress, she looked very big in the little kitchen. Here she became herself again and went about her work without speaking. I said nothing either, but I had often been here without many words being exchanged between us; they weren't necessary. She had an unintelligibly deep respect for me and my calling, and I was aware that I embarrassed her by standing at the door. Her son could stand there, and her late husband could have stood there, but the parish clerk ought not to; he should sit in the rocking chair and look at the album.

But after what had happened in church, I wanted very much to stand there for a moment, and be near the simple, ordinary things of the kitchen. A guest on the earth, a wanderer, needs to stand at the door of a kitchen. I stood there for a moment and stole a little of something that for me was a closed world, the world of the housewife at work in her kitchen, which had closed for me long ago with my right as a son to stand and watch his mother.

119

Marie took some sticks and shavings from the red-painted tinderbox and laid them in the kitchen range, then I struck a match and handed it to her without speaking. The shavings were soon ablaze and the sticks crackling, and there came the smell of burning pine. I had noticed how tidily the firewood was laid in the box; there was method and order with Marie. Certainly everything in the little blue kitchen was the worse for wear, but there was a difference between her ways and those of the house in which Kay lay ill. Kay's mother, Hansigne, hadn't many things either, and they were worn, but they had the look of her feebleness, her hopeless slovenliness, about them: they were dilapidated. Marie's things became dignified with wear. There was the sweetness of cleanliness in her home, like the fragrance of freshly washed and newly ironed clothes.

I didn't wish to embarrass her any longer, so I went into the room, sat myself in the rocking chair, and took the heavy album that I had looked at so many times before.

An old clock, a London chime, hangs ticking on the wall, its little door below the dial ornamented by a print of a hunting scene in oil colors. A blue-clad hunter kneels with his gun aimed at a red stag in the green forest. The stag, its eyes distorted, bounds high in the air; already it has been hit, but it has hung in its dying leap for many a long year. Hanging on the wall, there is also a southern oilprint of Christ, with his thorn-wreathed heart, radiating strong rays of light, painted on the outside of his cloak. Farther along hangs a shelf with coffee cups, Marie's hymnbook, and a brandy glass which has stood there since her husband was alive. There is a colored drawing of the three-masted schooner, *Margrete,* on which Johan, her husband, served when he was young. The waves are laid out as stylishly as the sticks in Marie's firewood box. On a chest

120

of drawers stands a beautiful tureen of old English pottery, and the shell of an armadillo, ingeniously shaped like a basket, in which she keeps her Christmas cards. There are family portraits, though all of her husband's family, in snail-shell frames and mother-of-pearl frames, and the many little things he had brought home in his younger days, when he was at sea, strange little things washed in here from the Seven Seas.

Marie comes in, opens one of the drawers, takes out a tablecloth, white as driven snow, fragrant, and lays it on the table. She goes out again, filling the doorframe. I can hear the saucepan, with the potatoes simmering, and smell the steam with its earthy flavor.

I have gradually come to realize a curious thing. Everything in the house originates from her husband's home. A little has been come by during the poverty of their married life, but there is nothing from Marie's home, though she came from much better circumstances than her husband, from an old farmstead on the mainland. I have heard from Oluf that once when his mother inherited some things, she had them sold over there. There's nothing here to remind her of her old home. She had deleted all traces of her youth, burnt her boats, and accepted her destiny. Yet there is one thing left—the heavy album of photographs.

Johan was some few years older than she, and already showed it when they were wed. She had to set to work harder than most fishermen's wives, but she did it. She was stronger than Johan; she wheeled the barrow for him, lugged the heaviest ends of the nets, and even went to sea with him, it is said. She went out to work by the side of him. He died of cancer before any of the children were confirmed. She worked harder then, washed for folk, worked in the turnip fields, and took whatever came to

121

hand to keep them. When the daughters grew up, they left the island, but she stayed. She has never left Sandö for more than a day at a time.

What is the thought, the reason behind it? That she will never disclose, nor perhaps could she, even if she wished to.

I sat in the rocking chair and glanced out through the window. Beyond the railings and the lilac bushes, the ground rises in gentle waves towards a hill, where there lies a half-plowed Bronze Age mound, with a drooping thorn bush growing on it. Farther to the right I could catch a glimpse of the idle sails of the windmill and the chimney pot of the dairy. Here is a little sample of all Sandö, a little, ordinary world.

Can nothing really be bigger than the hill out there? thought I. The hill is zero in number in geographical and astronomical tables, but look how it towers up to the sky! If one were to lie down in the field out there, it would be the largest thing one could possibly see, and would completely fill the view.

Then Sandö is large, too! thought I; and there is much that is unknown on the island. There are hidden masses of wild plants, species of seaweed and mosses, that I know nothing about. I constantly come across species of animal life that I have never noticed before. What does one really know of the island's soil, its geology? One has a very miserable knowledge of its history, too. What does one know of the people who have lived here in the past, and what does one really know of those that live here today? People are but fleeting grass. A puff of wind, a century-old wind, blows, and they are all dead and gone, and forgotten. And now a new generation lives, that knows nothing of those who once lived here and toiled and gossiped, laughed and cried, and cheated and helped each other. Another puff of wind and they are gone, eaten by worms and oblivion! Only a legend or two remain.

Yes, either the past life of a people vanishes completely, or only the smallest fragment of knowledge remains. What if I now did my bit to preserve a little of this knowledge? I sat in Marie's rocking chair in the corner of the room and got the idea that I would study and describe this island thoroughly, from the human societies to the mosses on the gravestones and the flea-lobsters on the beach. Yes, I got that idea sitting there, but perhaps it was a vain idea, Nathanael.

It might perhaps be that I realized in church today, all too strongly, that I was a complete stranger here on the island. But it could also be because I am sitting here in Oluf's mother's room, the room of someone who also once came as a stranger to the island, but who cut away the past and chose to stay and live here. For if anything stands firm on the island, if anything belongs entirely to the island, it is Marie, Oluf's mother.

Marie comes in and sets the plates on the white cloth. On her way out again she stops at the door and, looking at me over her shoulder, says: "You know, perhaps, that Annemari was here before she went to church?"

"No."

Couldn't we have a little peace even now! I thought. I could smell she was cooking eels in the pan. Why begin this trouble?

"She came to say that it was all over between Oluf and her."

"It's perhaps for the best," say I.

"Do you think so?" she said, and went out.

I sat and inhaled the odor from the kitchen. "Yes, now

123

shall I bow my face to the ground and gather flesh about my loins," as the Scriptures say. Now shall I in peace and quiet describe Sandö.

Marie came in with a bottle of pale ale, and placing it on the table said: "It's certainly the only good turn Annemari has ever done us!"

She went out again, and I thought that perhaps she was right. In any case, she's outright in her feelings, either hot or cold, without that lukewarmness which is the curse of so many people, especially thinking people. So that was the explanation of how it was possible for Marie and Annemari to be in the car together!

I began to glance through the photograph album. Hallo! There had been only one photograph of Annemari in Marie's album, put in by Oluf against strong opposition, no doubt. Now it was gone! Marie had removed it before going to church.

I looked further into the album, a sacred book of old family portraits of the last century. Faded, faint, they have turned a violet shade or a tobacco-brown, and have white spots on them, but they are beautiful. They are Marie's people, not only her family, but her stock: sturdy homeland farmers. Here are groups. The man, the master, in frock coat, is seated, one foot pushed forward; the woman, in a modest bonnet, stands behind with her flock of rigid children. Later, the photographs became larger, and were given a romantic background, a landscape with trees in a wood. Youths in soldiers' uniforms stand on idyllic bridges. In the groups, it is now the wife who sits and the husband stands, rising like a tower above her and the children.

Here is a picture of Johan, Marie's late husband, taken in his youth. A tall, sway-backed, bearded sailor, there is only the one picture of him.

124

Except for this, the album contains only blood-relations of Marie, in whose sturdy stock there are two types: a broadheaded, darker type, with a prominent nose and a hard eye—Marie's type—and a fairer, vaguer type, like Oluf, but in appearance he has turned out better than most of them.

There is an almost endless number of photographs of Marie's own children, mostly of Oluf. Things had never been so bad that she couldn't afford to send him over to the photographer each year. As a boy he has a slightly sheepish look, a swelling about the mouth, and wide-open, light blue eyes, but he is good-looking. From round about his eighteenth year the number of photographs of him increases. I have several of these myself. No doubt Oluf paid for them now, or sometimes Annemari perhaps. Like Oluf's mother she had a mania for photographs when she was a girl. They continually had to have photographs of him, but there's not a single one from the time he was grown up that is really like Oluf as he is, or as I know him. In the photographs he is not only tall, fair, and handsome in appearance, but he constantly has a strong, command-ing look, like a young chieftain. The mouth is firm, the eye sharp and keen. I've seen Oluf look like this only on one or two occasions, and then only for an instant. He isn't like this.

What is it I sit looking at? An idol: a mother's unreal dream of a youth; the enchantment of child-worship possi-bly made him look like this to her—a mother's family god! Marie broke with everything in her former life; nothing of her past was any longer allowed to exist, but she carried hidden within her a family deity. At last I've come to realize it, and it seems to me that I've stepped into a pagan rite, where humans are sacrificed.

But twice during the same day I saw that look in Oluf's

eyes. It was the day he came home again to Sandö, after Niels was drowned and he himself had swum to Golö Reef. We'd heard about it on the radio, and now he was coming on the mailboat, and everyone who could walk, or even crawl, was down at the boat to meet him. I was there with Annemari. At that time she was expecting her baby, and looked even more worried now than she did the day Oluf and Niels capsized.

There were several people standing on the steamer's foredeck, but Oluf stayed below until the ship came alongside. Then he came bounding up, pushing his way through, and in one leap was over the gunwale and on to the wharf. Tall, pale, he stood almost paralyzed at the sight of so many people, then Annemari went to him, leaning against him, crying. He twisted his face and looked at me over her head, and then he had that look.

"Where is she—mother?" he asked. She wasn't there.

He set off home.

Annemari and I followed him over the cliff, as well as she could. He was walking away with long strides past the houses. At last we got to the top of the cliff and Annemari stopped for breath. We could see the road up to his mother's house. Oluf was halfway there; he was running, bounding over the newly sown fields where little shoots were shining, running like a wild animal.

"Look!" exclaimed Annemari, though we were both standing watching.

"I understand him so well," she declared.

After a short while she said it again, but it sounded as if she didn't understand him.

And I thought, as we stood there watching him running home: there is someone running after him, someone right on his heels!

126

Towards evening, they came to school to see me, the two of them, Annemari and he. There wasn't a great deal to notice. She sat down and took out some sewing, while Oluf stood and fiddled with my books on the shelves. I went out into the kitchen to put some water on.

When I came back I got the instruments out. I handed him my violin, because he plays it better than his own, so that I've often thought of giving it to him, but have never done so. I took the cello and began to look among some old music that lies littering the place, but he had tuned the violin and began to play. It's a bad habit of his to want to play a piece by heart before he has practiced it sufficiently. He has talent, without being exceptional, and has perhaps had his dreams about playing. I ought, perhaps, to have run about here and there, to see if I could find someone to support him while he went to the mainland to study music properly. He was playing the Slavonic melody of Rimsky-Korsakov, "The Czar's Bride."

He broke off and turned to Annemari: "I went in to look at an automatic record-player when I was over there. Thirty pounds."

"It would be lovely," she answered, without looking up.

He began playing again; broke off a second time; laid the violin and bow carefully on the table.

"It's no use!" he said, and walked to the window, where he stood looking out, with his back towards us. It was dark outside.

A long minute passed. Annemari didn't raise her head to look at me, and I thought it was extraordinarily fine of her.

"Why must it be like this, sir?" he asked, without moving. He usually called me by my Christian name, though

127

it had taken him a long time to get used to it. This present form of addressing me was proud and challenging.

"I don't know, Oluf."

"Was I better than Niels, perhaps?"

"No."

"Thanks," said he, and laughed a bit. He slowly drew the blind down, then let go of it. It flew up with a smack, and Annemari was startled.

"Are you both aware that I killed him, out there?"

Annemari bent forward and covered her face.

"Are you aware of it?"

"Yes, I knew it."

"You don't know what you are talking about, Johannes," said he, with his back towards me.

"I know you are a damned idiot!" I said.

That turned him round, turned him face to face with me! He knit his brow and glared, while his large hands slowly clenched.

"Don't think you can say just what you like!" he uttered with difficulty.

"Shut up!" I said. "You're a fool! I could easily see that you've had Niels close on your heels ever since. And why? Because you couldn't bring him with you. You got hold of him, but Niels can hardly swim and lost his head. He drags you down, so you free yourself. It's nothing to become affected about!"

"But I fought with him, with Niels!"

"Yes, he dragged you down, and the boat drifted away so that you couldn't reach it."

"It was impossible," he said, "impossible!"

"Of course, because the boat drifted away from you," I said. "You couldn't get him to the boat. Impossible, in that sea! There isn't a man living who could have done it, who could have saved him. I won't hear any more of your silly talk!"

"Yes, but it is all lies what I told them," said he. "They asked questions and questions and questions! I said he went straight to the bottom. It's a lie, for I had hold of him. But they asked and asked!"

"Shut your damned mouth," I ordered, "and sit down! Sit down!"

He sat down on a chair near the window, breathing heavily and quickly.

"This is the last time we will hear a word about this matter," I said, "once and for all! You could, of course, in a grand manner, have gone to the bottom with him. Good gracious! We should never have guessed how finely you had behaved, and a little fatherless child would have been born into the world! Yes, it would indeed have been ideal! I won't hear another word of that damned nonsense!"

He sat with his back half turned and looked out. Yes, he had had a ghost behind him all this time, a terror, even while he was swimming, otherwise he would never have reached Golö Reef. And then he had sat alone for two nights on the reef.

"Don't sit there lolling about!" I said to Annemari; "get out and make the coffee! The water is boiling away."

"Yes," she murmured and hurried out.

I turned the radio on, pottered about, mumbling angrily to myself. I'd said it all to get the upper hand of him, but it wouldn't have gone so easily if I hadn't got exasperated myself.

There was some music on the radio, I cannot remember what.

Oluf came over and sat himself in my chair. He eased

himself up again and took the tobacco jar from the table, then he settled down and began to fill his pipe.

"Yes, yes," he said.

After the accident with Niels, Oluf's drowsiness increased, and the affair between Annemari and him came to nothing, even though she had little Tom.

VIII

SUNDAY afternoon.

I had hoped to have the rest of the day to myself, to think over the idea that I had formed in Oluf's mother's house, namely, to make a careful study of the people and the natural history of Sandö, but of course I got no peace.

I left Oluf's mother early after dinner. Crossing over the fields, which didn't do my Sunday shoes much good, I went to see if the partridges were still somewhere near the spot where I'd come across them in the fog on Friday.

The haze over the island was saturated with light. But you couldn't push a stick more than a couple of inches into the plowed earth. Below the surface it was still hard with frost. The shining meadows were drenched, but the water trickled away over the surface without sinking, draining away to the shore. It's a pity, for the land hasn't had enough rain.

I saw nothing of the partridges, but found the first colts-foot, a drowsy, wool-covered little fellow, no longer in the neck than Henry VIII of England.

Bödvar Bjarke was out looking at his winter rye, and wailing about the poorness of it. Bjarke is not his real name; he got it from one of the legends told at school. And, of course, he has seldom had such beautiful dark rye, for it has been well protected by the snow this year.

He told me that everyone was expecting the boat to arrive tomorrow morning at the latest, perhaps even earlier. It was mainly brash that lay in the seaway out towards the east, and two large boats had been seen to pass through it easily.

I hurried home. Poor Pigro was so heavy with sleep that he could hardly be bothered to stick his aristocratic nose out of doors. It was now that I was hoping to sit in peace and quiet and turn over in my mind the idea of writing an account of Sandö. So I lit the stove in the schoolroom, as I always work best there. But Bödvar's information about the boat disturbed my peace of mind. I rang up the lighthouse and was told by the assistant that the mail boat would try to reach Tulö this afternoon. If it got through, it would try to come on to Sandö later in the afternoon, or perhaps tonight. It must try to get through as early as possible, there was so much stuff waiting in storage on both sides.

The news made things no easier for me. That Oluf would arrive by the first boat, whenever it might be, I was certain. No doubt he was already sitting waiting in the harbor, over on the mainland.

It was no more than I'd expected all along, yet it disturbed me and I had to do something, so I rang up Frederik at the Headlands.

Now, of course, I was disturbing that busy man who had all the world to care for! But had Rigmor spoken to him about little Kay? I would just like to know if it was possible for them to take him in the car?

Oh, yes, Rigmor had hardly spoken about anything else, and, of course, he would gladly take the lad, but Rigmor had said something about going over to the mainland in a day or so with the car, and that wasn't possible—not with the car. He had trouble enough with the skipper at ordinary times when he wanted to take the car over, but for the first few days there wouldn't be room for it on the boat.

I didn't mean him to take the boy over in his car, I told him; if he would only run Kay down to the boat, I should be glad.

Goodness gracious, he would gladly run the lad to the end of the world! Frederik answered; but it wasn't much fun having the cursed car! He knew well enough that we all quietly laughed at his having a car here on the island. Originally, it was intended that the car should stay over in the town, but he was as pleased as a child with a new toy when he brought it over in the autumn. But he hadn't had any real pleasure out of it; he was sick of the damned thing! And did I know that he'd been sitting since eight o'clock this morning trying to find a damned three pennies that he was out in the tax accounts?

No; I was sorry about it. I knew that an error of three pennies in the accounts would worry Frederik as much as if it had been a million crowns.

"But you can tell them that I'll take the boy over to the sanatorium on Tuesday. Good-bye!"

Rigmor's voice followed his immediately—she had obviously been standing by his side. She said Frederik had gone back to look for the three pennies. "but if I know him, you had better be prepared for his leaving in the morning, if he can. We should very much like to take Kay."

"It's frightfully good of you both," I said.

"I love you," she said.

"And I you," I answered. The girl at the exchange would be cocking her ears now, I thought.

"Then you will come tonight?" she invited.

"No," I answered, "I must write a topographical work on Sandö."

"I've rung the inn and spoken to Elna," said Rigmor, "she is free this afternoon but not tonight. It's a pity, but she can't come."

"Then it's out of the question," I said.

"I love you," she said again.

"Yes, and I love you too," I answered.

"What use is it though?" she asked.

133

"What do you expect to thrive in this callous sand?" I replied.

"Heavens!" she exclaimed, "I've some cakes browning in the oven!"

I cycled over to the house below the Sand Hills. It was after two o'clock, but Anders and Hansigne were sitting with the children in the kitchen, having their dinner. In front of each of them was a little pile of potato peelings. The air was steaming hot and there was an unpleasant smell of uncleanliness. Poor Hansigne looked at me, scared out of her wits! As a woman she will be no good at anything until she is old and has some of her burdens lifted from her. She has too many of them and she's afraid of them. When she is old a kind of sweetness will grow over her, I think; she will blossom, beautiful but late, like many other poor souls whose lives are made up of worry and anxiety, and fear and dread of not being able to please others. Now she was worried, because everything was so untidy and she dared not offer me anything. But the bearded Anders went on quietly with his eating.

"It was the spruce trees," I said, "but no doubt you have remembered about them?"

"I am going to begin felling them in the morning, at seven o'clock," answered Anders.

My lovely spruce trees! But a promise is a promise.

Then I told them that Kay might be taken to the sanatorium the next day.

"I won't have the boy taken by those people at the Headlands," said Anders; "I won't be under any obligation to them. Besides, I have been paying sick-benefit contributions and can have him taken by the association."

Hansigne's face changed as though a whirlwind had blown over it. At first she was humbly delighted that Kay should ride in the fine car, but now all the lines of anxiety showed in her ruined young face.

"May I remind you, Anders," said I, "that you and I had a few words when Kay first began to be unwell, and I've some say in this matter?"

"I know well enough that I was against it, schoolmaster," replied Anders, "but I agreed afterwards to let Kay go; I also said that he wouldn't go with them from the Headlands."

"You needn't worry yourself about them," I said. "I'll make the arrangements. But I dare say you've already noticed that there aren't so many folk who dare to come near you. Your children notice it in school, too, and it will go on like that, Anders. That's why I want Frederik at the Headlands to take Kay, it will make an impression on the other folk."

Finally he agreed. I peeped in at Kay, who was lying in a reeking hot atmosphere. I'd been afraid that they would all get it, and it hasn't been easy to get them to do the right thing, but up to the present only Kay has been affected.

I had one or two annuals of the National Museum with me, together with a slightly defective flint axe, which I had found earlier in the winter. Kay already has a small collection of antiquities.

"I wonder if there is any trace of single grave burial on the island?" Kay asked.

"Not that I know of," I answered, "but Sandö has never been properly investigated. But listen! I've just decided that we must study the island more thoroughly. When you come home again you will have to help me with it."

"Do you think it will be long?" he asked. Kay is delicate in the face, tender as an anemone now: a gifted boy, good to talk to. I shall miss him.

135

"A year, perhaps, but we have said that before," I answer; "but they have a lot of books at those places, and besides, we can always send you one or two."

"About antiquity," he said.

I noticed Anders, Kay's father. He often listens with a shy smile while his intelligent son is talking, but today he sits in his chair, ugly and gloomy, with a strange, glazed look. Feeling his poverty, perhaps. Another steals his boy during his last day here. Anders knows a lot about the soil, the sun, and the birds, but he can't express himself. He can go outside and show you, but he can no longer take Kay out and show him anything, thus he has nothing to say to the lad.

I stayed no longer.

It was cozy in the schoolroom when I got back. I took some books and one or two notebooks in with me. Here I become almost another person.

First of all, I would gather together all I could find published about Sandö, but that wasn't much. After that, I would arrange my own dispersed notes that I've written throughout the years I've been here. Yes, perhaps it is a vain idea, but Kay lies thinking now about when he will be helping me.

I turned to the first page of a new notebook, and at the top wrote the title, short and sweet: "Sandö," and underneath: "By Johannes Vig."

But I wrote no more, Nathanael.

I don't know if you have these moments; they are so rare that I've experienced only two of them in the whole of my life—moments when it seems that everything opens out in front of you, lies absolutely open. Here in the schoolroom was such a moment.

But I ought to begin at the beginning. I started to laugh when I saw my name at the top of the first page in the notebook, "By Johannes Vig." In an unthinking moment I had disclosed my vanity, and noticing it, I was immediately attacked by the light gaiety that precedes the moment in which the mind is caught by dark, somber thoughts.

I recollected those evil minutes in church, when I felt possessed of the Devil. I had, perhaps, prepared myself to be so possessed. I had felt half-hearted, empty, like a stranger, a guest of the moment. So it happened.

Evil recollections are gregarious, they come in flocks. I recalled many such thoughts. I have tampered with the destinies of people, have changed their fates. Perhaps no one can help doing it. But had I done it as a man, loving and hating, prompted by his heart? Or had I done it for the sake of convenience or as a pastime, as it might be done by a visitor or a stranger?

You find, perhaps, that these questions aren't clear, Nathanael, but on these occasions thoughts are apt to be confused.

I sat and looked round the schoolroom. Faced by a keen critic, my friend, my only defense must lie here in the schoolroom. The children like to come here and they learn something. There are interesting little things in this room, curious things. There's the wall newspaper, the "Sandö Times," beside the door. There are the museum and the art collection, each in its little cupboard. There's the exhibition on the back wall, above the high wainscot of Rasmus Sandbjerg's painted roses. There are the children's own drawings, which they've framed themselves; we change these from time to time, and I've thought it a good idea; but perhaps it's deceitful, as I've made them believe that other people will be interested in their work. And underneath them is the library, the little collection of books we have bought by working hard to scrape a little money together. Perhaps that is a fraud, too! Yes, the whole thing is perhaps a swindle, organized in an interesting and pleasant way, so that a certain person may have a comfortable time here during his visit to the island.

And there are the school desks, which the boys have carved throughout the years with names and dates. Our former pastor didn't like it, and in his very witty way reproached me for allowing it. I said to him: "Sandö has no art, no runic stone, no history. The only artistic and historic writing we have is what is carved in these desks here. Look, here you can see a galleass and the name 'Niels Jensen.' It is all that is left of Niels; it is his memorial."

And as I sat here, nursing my doubts, it happened, Nathanael; the schoolroom opened up to me as it has never opened before. How? I can't explain. But I thought it spoke to me, and I promised it to stay on here as long as I can. Yes, it blessed its servant, I thought.

I believe I sat there a long time without really thinking, and then, gradually, I realized that someone had been knocking at the outer door.

It was the young engineer, Harry, to give him his real name, with a long roll under his arm. I was more annoyed than gracious, partly because I was being disturbed, and partly because I'd forgotten that I had myself invited him. I showed him into the schoolroom while I tidied up a little in my own room. When I went back to the schoolroom, he was standing with the roll under his arm, peering into the bird case.

"I got curious," he said; "but why do you put a cover in front of the case?"

"Well, why did you get curious?" I said.

"Is it a pedagogic trick?" he asked.

"Just a bit of tomfoolery," I answered.

"Have you shot all the birds yourself?"

"Some of them. But we have stuffed them all ourselves."

"Is that one a woodcock?" he asked.

"No, it's a curlew, the large curlew. It was caught along by The Hook, near to where I met you last night. Here is the woodcock."

"I thought the woodcock was a larger bird," he said.

"It looks larger when it flies up just in front of you. It is a magic bird."

"When does the woodcock come?"

"Today," I said, "when Christ casts out the unclean spirit—or rather tonight, the woodcock migrates at night, and alone, preferably in misty weather."

"Do you think yourself that it will come tonight?" he asked, smiling.

"I am sure," I answered; "but look at the bird! Look at its long, sad beak and its remarkably vigilant head! The colors have faded, however: expert taxidermists can preserve the colors, but I haven't been able to do so; but you can guess what they were like—the golden gleam, and the deep brown. The eyes, however, aren't the right ones, I've had to use the eyes of a bird of prey until I'm able to get the proper ones. The woodcock has large, dark eyes, which merge into the half-light of the woods. There have been times when I was looking for it and it stood staring me in the face for a long time, but I didn't see it until it got up."

"Did you shoot it then?"

"Yes, I did."

"I couldn't bear to," he said, and his voice began to quiver.

"Really," said I.

"Yes, forgive me," said he, "but hunting. . .! No, I couldn't—I couldn't kill or hurt a wild creature unnecessarily."

139

"Of course," said I, "I understand perfectly. I've had lots of good, well-meaning pamphlets against hunting sent to me. Yet it's well known that wild life increases where there are careful hunters; but there's no advantage to be gained by discussing it here."

Resting his chin on one end of his long roll, and still looking at the bird case, he said, almost hesitatingly: "I was only once out shooting, and that was when I was a youngster. I enjoyed it. But since then I've had to drag a young fellow, who was shot in the stomach, through backyards, over a hoarding, and up the stairs to a fourth floor, to prevent them from getting him, and to do it I had to shoot down three men on the way, men who stood staring me in the face, just like you and the woodcock."

I put the bird back in the case, closed it, and drew the cover over it again. When I turned round he lowered his eyes, began to untie the string round the roll, fumbled with it, and drew it into a knot. To distract my attention, he looked round the room and said: "This is a very pleasant schoolroom . . . but I can't understand why you've come out here, to bury yourself in this loneliness."

"Loneliness!" thought I—sounded exaggerated, not his usual pitch of voice, either. He's uncertain, begins to withdraw into himself again.

"I had to," I said; "an affair—an awkward business."

"Oh!" said he, and bent down, fiddled with the knot in the string. When I offered him a cigarette, he dropped the roll awkwardly on to the floor, bent down quickly to pick it up, and then straightened up again, with a dark, vexed expression which soon passed, however. But his annoyance had given him back his confidence and he cut the string.

The roll turned out to be a large, clear map of Sandö. The paper was pasted on linen, fastened to rollers at the ends.

140

"If it's any use to you, I should like to be allowed to present it to the school," he said. "I've had plenty of time on my hands, so I amused myself by remeasuring a good deal of the island. I drew a new map for the company and made one for the school, with heavier lines, while I was at it."

I thanked him and complimented him on the map, which was a good bit of work, large and clear, so that the children could see each house on the island without getting up from their places. I was glad to have it, and we knelt before it on the floor, studying its detail for a long time.

Then we went into my room and I got out a couple of glasses. He had become more free in manner and began to tell me something of his plans. He had been with his firm for three years, but hadn't been given enough outside work to do. He wanted to go abroad, especially to take part in some big project, in a country which was technically undeveloped. He was, if anything, a socialist, and believed in technical science as an instrument for creating a better and more equitable society. He talked eagerly and energetically about it.

"Naturally, you think that technical science has become the master of man!" he said. "I've read it, and heard it said, thousands of times! But do you think you can stop development? Is there anything else we can do, except to work and work, and keep it under control and within reason? Do you know of any other way out? I suppose you are one of those who preach that people, people of today, must be changed from inside if the world is to be saved, aren't you? But where are the results? It goes devilishly slow that way!"

"And swimmingly by the other," I said; "but what makes you suppose that I believe as you say I do?"

"I nearly said that I can smell it a mile away," he said.

141

"Excuse my speaking so frankly, but I think you are man enough to take it. You are a reactionary—in the nicest way, of course! Take your room here—understand me rightly, I envy you really—classical literature, books that are actually read, picturesque disorder, instruments, beautiful reproductions; but, if I may be blunt, your existence and your ideas remind me of an old drawer that smells of lavender when it is opened."

"Bravo!"

"Why do you say 'bravo'?" he asked.

"I like your striking metaphor," I said; "I must remember to make a note of it. But you know nothing about me."

"I only know," he said, "that people like myself must work with something concrete. We can't just sit around expecting that thinking will do anything for us. I've just told you about something that happened during the occupation, something I never thought I should speak about. Yes, I was in it; I shot; I don't regret it, it's simply a fact. I don't know if I could do it again, but I just won't think about doing it again! I will work, build, produce. Can't you understand? I must!"

He walked backwards and forwards behind me, while I filled the glasses again.

"Yes, I shot," he said again, "but I can't, God help me, sit down and go on thinking about it, and expect to get any mental recreation out of it, or whatever it is you call it. I once tried this business of sitting still and thinking. It nearly drove me mad. No, we have only one way out, that is to work and go on working, believing in what we do."

He sat down, emptied his glass, and said: "I didn't mean to talk like that. It must be a kind of island madness—is there such a thing?"

"Yes," I answered. I heard Pigro whimpering outside

142

the door and went to let him in. I had hardly sat down again before he said: "If you hadn't mentioned it last night, that she ... Annemari had broken it off with the other fellow, I shouldn't talk about it now, but I was glad to hear it."

Oh, oh! I thought, that was strange!

"Why have you always tried to—to fill her—in fact, to prevent it? To be against me?"

"To drive her into your arms," I said; "that's how it's done. I'm a little bit of a schoolmaster, you know!"

"You're joking again," he said. "After all, Annemari isn't a child. She has a child herself, but otherwise she is independent, except that you have an influence over her. Why have I all along had to come up against this ghost, the other man? He has no rights!"

"No," I said, "not an absent ghost away in a sleeper factory."

"You like to jest," he said.

"Yes, I'm very fond of it."

He got up and walked over towards the window, and stood on the very spot where Oluf had stood when he talked about Niels's death, only it was bright daylight outside now.

"Annemari is going away with me," he said; "she mustn't be kept down any longer. It's true that at first I didn't intend anything serious with Annemari. I was living at the inn and the evenings were damned long and lonely, and here was a nice-looking girl, so why not? I thought she was a little ... prudish, perhaps—betrothed in the grand manner; but perhaps the girls on the island are like that, I thought, and actually I wasn't sorry about it. Then it became serious. I will take Annemari away with me!"

"Why do you stand there telling me all this?" I asked. "She is free!"

"There's a shadow!" he said. "A damned shadow that I want rid of! I won't beg anything from you, but it's from you it comes—the past; damned morbidness!"

What a difference there is in people, I thought. This man is a fine fellow, but Oluf is finer. Oluf has visited me almost daily for seven years and we've talked about many things, but never about his feelings, never about Anne-mari.

"I'm sorry I'm so glad to have that good map!" I said.

"Why?" he asked.

"Because it puts me under an obligation to you, and I can't say what I would otherwise."

"Don't let that prevent you," he said with an acid smile. "I didn't give it to you, but to the school."

"That relieves me," I answered, "but I thank you again on behalf of the school. We shall derive much pleasure from it. You might think what I'm doing is rather lav-ender-like: I salute you, have respect for you and for what you would like to do; but, finally, I will say, you can go to hell!"

"Thanks," he said, smiling.

"Thank yourself," I answered.

He strode erectly past me and out.

I heard him talking to someone in the front garden. When I opened the outer door, I saw him standing talking to Elna, the girl at the inn. She was made up and looked fairly pretty.

It looked as if she was slightly taken up with him. Then I had a wicked thought—he had lived all the time at the inn, hadn't he?

They both looked towards me and smiled.

"Perhaps you would rather I didn't come today?" suggested Elna.

"No," I said; "come right in!"

He nodded and called: "Thanks for everything!"

144

"Thank yourself," I said. He strode out through the gate with his head high in the air. He was both taller and broader since his visit; at least, he looked it.

"You can help me to make the coffee, Elna," I said.

The kitchen makes a good confessional for a woman. She chatted away easily and cheerfully, quite differently from the night she confided to me that she was going to have a baby. It was a young man she had met over in the town during the autumn. She had come to like him a good deal and believed that he was serious too, but lately she had begun to have her doubts. Otherwise, he might at least have telephoned to her once, during the long time the ice had closed the island, but she hadn't heard a single word from him.

We sat and talked, she sitting on the kitchen table, I on the chair, while we drank our coffee. I said: "March, April, it will do fine in May. You can give your notice in for May. I could just do with a more reliable help than Margrete in the house. Then you can move in here in May, if you want to."

I'm constantly jumping into things, I thought to myself, and making a lot of trouble for myself, a whole load of difficulties.

She sat quietly for a minute or two, then she broke down, as if struck by a flail, and heavens above, what tears there were in that big, hulking girl!

IX

SUNDAY night was the spring ball at the Headlands. All the evening I expected Oluf to turn up, like the joker in a game of cards.

But late on Sunday afternoon, as it was turning dark, I was sitting here in my room, thinking over what had happened. I had hoped for a quiet afternoon so that I could toy with my new idea of writing about Sandö. Instead, there was nothing but disturbance and trouble.

That's how it is with us, Nathanael. One looks forward to a little peace, a little peace and quietness to oneself, but what happens? I give up! I will look for peace no longer, my friend, not real peace. I will impose upon myself no longer, instead I will choose to expect unrest and discord.

> The raven flies at even,
> It may not fly by day.
> It is a bird of ill luck,
> No good can come its way.

But perhaps you've already seen through my little game, Nathanael, and are amused by it? You say: "Look here, Johannes, you're deceiving yourself again, already! You're led away by an old rhyme. You say you will choose to expect unrest and emotional discord, but wait until tomorrow, when you're in a different mood! You will sit back again and become the tourist in life, the guest of the moment, hoping again for peace and quiet. Just wait and see!"

Yes, you are right! You're always so right. One never knows what one will do tomorrow.

146

However, I'm determined to try to live by my experience that one must expect to have trouble, that it's one's lot in life to have trouble. And one thing is certain, Nathanael—the past comes again, for the past is a hound, a beagle always on the trail. Beagles are short-legged and slow, but they never lose the trail. The hare or fox may make off a long way ahead, and play tricks to obscure the trail, but the beagles always catch up again. The fox makes off again, far ahead, but the beagles catch up again. The past always catches up again!

On one of the school desks there has been carved, with a Finnish dagger, the name "Niels Jensen." Niels did it as a boy. Since then he has sailed out and been drowned. I've seen this name every day for years, but it's only now that I've perhaps come to realize how it really is carved. It stands carved in my own flesh. Stretch your hand out, Nathanael, and look at it. Imagine to yourself that you, with that hand, could as easily as anything have held Niels back that time, that you could have stopped him and Oluf by a bend of the finger.

Yes, I sat brooding as the darkness came. Elna had been here and had gone home again to the inn. How she cried, that sulky big girl, I thought she would never dry out again! Gracious me, how she thawed; she must have wept all her frozen youth out of her! And just because I had made the offer for her to come and live here and have her baby. Not only was Elna's gratitude greater than my kindness, but I'm not sure that there was any kindness in it, Nathanael. It was only an idea. One gets an idea and asks a man to come and fell the spruce trees, the lovely spruce trees! One gets another idea and offers a home to a poor, pregnant girl, and with it destroys one's own sweet loneliness.

Certainly it was the right thing to do, to help the girl,

147

and through it to choose trouble—for it will bring a lot of trouble and difficulty. There will, no doubt, be some who will think that I've gone too far again, taking the fat barmaid into my home. Let them, I can hit back.

But was it done out of goodness? I'll leave you to find the answer, my friend, I can't make it out myself. But before Elna came I had another guest, the engineer, and while it's true we fell out, I must admit he seemed a very fine fellow; and he's going to take Annemari with him, yes, he's going to take her! Yet he was rather naïve when he confessed there was a little shadow between them. "A shadow!" he said, and became quite emotional. What sort of shadow can it be between them, Nathanael? Perhaps it's Annemari's slightly old-fashioned and rather troublesome conscience. She will never feel herself quite free until she has settled up properly with Oluf.

In the stillness, I sat thinking about this shadow, until there came a wild, youthful vigor from it. I thought to myself I would do the opposite to what people would expect me to do—I would burn my boats! So I said to Elna she could come here in May, and afterwards I told her she needn't keep it a secret.

It was dark outside now, and had perhaps been dark for a long time. I'd noticed Pigro's shuffling and whimpering beside the door for some time; once he had barked, but I hadn't bothered myself much about it.

But now there was a disturbance at the outer door, and then a knock. It was Mrs. Höst, Annemari's mother. Behind her glasses, her eyes gaped up in terror towards the lamp in the passage, but there's nearly always the look of catastrophe in Mrs. Höst's eyes.

"Is little Tom not here? Oh, God! Oh, God!" she panted, and I had to catch hold of her. "Annemari has gone out and left us to look after him. Oh, God!" she wailed.

148

I had to speak sharply to Pigro as I called him in; he was fussing around in the garden in the dark. Then I pulled on my high boots.

"You must find him for us, parish clerk, you must!" she cried. It did me good to hear her speak so distractedly, and address me by my church title.

Pigro was so excited I had to hold him by the collar as we hurried over to the shop. Höst himself and his pale-faced assistant had been round the houses inquiring. Little Tom had been missing for nearly an hour. I sent the assistant along the road towards the church, and I got hold of one of Tom's vests to give Pigro the scent. When I let the dog loose he disappeared like the wind into the dark. That was silly and not like Pigro. I got him whistled back, and then he set off beautifully on the trail and I was able to follow him easily. But the grocer and his wife couldn't keep up with us so I shouted to them they had better go home.

The trail led straight to my own doorway, and then backwards and forwards under my window; then into the garden, through the spruce, and out into the fields in large, winding curves. It was quite dark. Then I thought: now I'm beginning to see a pattern in all that's happening; if little Tom meets with a disaster the pattern will be complete!

But there was nothing the matter with Tom when Pigro found him, standing at the edge of the marl-pit down in Bödvar's field. The water was shining faintly and he had thrown a lot of soil into it, he said. Little Tom was covered with mud. Pigro danced around, licking him, and today Tom wasn't displeased by it. I lifted him up into my arms.

"Wanted to see the partridges!" he said, when I asked him. He wanted to see the partridges I had promised to show him, but I'd been too busy.

"Why weren't you at home?" he asked. So I'd been sitting there with my profound thoughts and hadn't been at home to my little guest! And I haven't said much, either, about little Tom in these pages, though I'm with him a good deal, usually.

He put his arms round my neck and I held him tightly to me as I walked. There was a raw breeze, with low clouds in the distance.

I stayed for a while at Höst's, playing with Tom till he had to go to bed. Mrs. Höst was first to recover from the shock, because she could get relief in sighing and wailing, excitement and tears. She talked about all the possible things that could have happened, all the dangers that had threatened the little one. The half-deaf grocer sat at the table, looking through some old newspapers; now and then he gave a shudder as though he was freezing. He is a stout, good-looking man in the fifties, bald, with little dark curls at the back of his head.

Mrs. Höst began to talk softly about Harry, that fine fellow, and how it would soon come to something. Wasn't he a grand young man? Didn't I think this, and didn't I think that? Yes, and Oluf?—what about him? But he'd made his bed and must lie on it.

"What's that you're saying about Oluf?" demanded Höst, glaring over his spectacles.

"We were only saying how good Oluf is to his mother," said Mrs. Höst, full of affection, but shameless.

As I walked home, I could hear the music at the Headlands.

It was no good sitting alone after what had happened, so I set off for the Headlands. Half-way there I turned back again, but turned again and walked on. The windows were shining like magic through the trees. The fairies were having a party. I stood for a while outside, peering through the windows. There was a good crowd of elves,

150

young and old. Rigmor walked through the rooms, ashen-pale but beautiful.

The early spring ball is an old custom on the island. I like to think that as a custom it goes a long way back into the past, perhaps to the time when the goddess of fertility was worshiped on Western Hill. The people on the island save some of their ale and other good drinks for this night. It's also an old custom to hold it at the Headlands, formerly in the barn, but Frederik is generous and fond of the grand gesture. He would like to be the beloved chieftain and turn our molehill upside-down; we must all be chickens under his tender wings. Since he has been master the ball has always been held in the large house, but according to custom the guests still bring a little something to eat and drink with them and hand it into the kitchen. However, Frederik really supplies all that's needed and there's always ample.

Now I enter the fairy-house.

A woman's voice whispers something behind me.

"I can't hear what you say, Fairy Queen. What a noise they're making!"

"The first dance is mine, Johannes!"

"They're all yours, Fairy Queen!"

"I must hurry off, but I'll be straight back! Open a window! We can hardly breathe for smoke."

"Need we breathe?"

"Have you had anything to drink?"

"Not yet, but I would like something!"

"I'll bring it. I'll be straight back!"

"We want a fourth at this table; sit here, parish clerk!"

"You're too good for me! Besides, I want to dance. It sounds more exciting in the hall, I'm going in there!"

"You'd better sit here and stay with the old folks."

"Just a minute, I'm thirsty."

"You're always thirsty!"

151

"Do you know the parish clerk wouldn't believe that the woodcock comes when Christ drives out the unclean spirit? He wouldn't believe me!"

"Thou shalt not bear false witness against thy neighbor, Kristian: I firmly believe it. The woodcock has come today."

"Where did you see it?"

"Over in church. It was a woodcock as sure as I was standing there!"

"The schoolmaster is not exactly teetotal, you know!"

"But did you not think ... I thought it was a bit queer in church."

Why do they suddenly go quiet, so that there's a little island of stillness in all the talk and noise around them? What does it mean?

"Don't you worry about it. You asked Lena, Erik's widow; whom better could you ask?"

"That's right, whom better could he have asked, Robert?"

"Here you are, Johannes! I'll be back in a moment—but you haven't opened any of the windows yet!"

"I like smoke and fog, my dear."

"I'll be straight back. Wait for me!"

"Your good health, all of you!"

"Good health, parish clerk, good health!"

"Have you been to see Peter's shooting-boat?"

"No bid!" "No bid!" "One heart!" "No bid!" "Two spades!" "No bid!" "Four spades!"

"Speak louder, Valdemar, I can't hear you. Was it Peter's boat you were talking about?"

"Thanks, a glass here!" "And one here!" "Confound it, you're not opening with hearts?" "Yes, it's spring again, the wagtail is here."

"The right thing to do is to draw the hearts first!"

"I'll bet there's a truck-load of beer standing on the quay!"

"It's Peter's boat I mean, schoolmaster. He's painted it so bright the angels are singing about it! Green, with white edging."

"We'll have to put up a memorial to that boat! Why aren't you playing your concertina tonight, Valdemar?"

"They have the phonograph; when they're tired of the records I'll play."

"That will be never, Valdemar. It's all mechanical music now. You can go out and dig a grave for your concertina!"

"Oluf and I used to play well together, but he had some life in him then. You wouldn't think there was any life in him now, but there is! If only he and I could play again! But he won't come any more."

"Yes, he will. He'll be here tonight, and then the fun will start!"

"What do you mean, schoolmaster?"

"The parish clerk can tell you my rye has never been so poor. Prices will soar like the larks!" "We'll have to do what they are doing in other places, get a State loan for bigger cutters and go out into the North Sea." "You can see it, can't you? She's like that!"

"There were already two of them, and Elna at the inn makes the third." "Never in the world!" "Really!" "But what else could you expect?" "That makes two legitimate and one illegitimate, two up and one to carry!"

"Now, Johannes, I am ready!"

"Where has Frederik got to tonight?"

"He's sitting playing cards in the study, with his cowman, a young fisherman, and another man. You know Frederik has to show how democratic he is when there's a party."

"Frederik has higher aims than we, Rigmor."

153

"And he talks all the time about the three pennies he can't find in the tax accounts—tells everybody! This afternoon I discovered him sitting crying at his writing desk, over the three pennies."

"I can well believe it, Rigmor. What did you do?"

"Consoled him, of course."

"What should we do? Where shall we go?"

"Shall we go outside? Out on to the terrace? There's nobody in the room facing the garden. I've rushed backwards and forwards to the kitchen; I'm so hot, and all that smoke!"

"You have hardly anything on, you'll catch cold out here."

"This is lovely! I won't catch anything, I wish I could!"

"You can look at the stars and wish."

"What a lot there are, Johannes! And how they shine!"

"I had a strange experience in the schoolroom today, Rigmor."

"Tell me about it! I never hear anything. Put your arm round me!"

"Could you imagine yourself embraced by your kitchen?"

"Not by my kitchen!"

"You shouldn't say that: but it was almost like that with the schoolroom—I can't properly explain it."

"Try, though, Johannes! I always tell you a lot of things over the telephone; I can never tell you all I would like to, however!"

"Say whatever you like, it couldn't spoil our reputations."

"Have I a bad reputation, Johannes?"

"You have! And it wouldn't surprise anybody if you started to do something else unusual, either!"

"What are you thinking of, my dear?"

"You could do a lot of really good things, especially for

154

folks who are in a bad way. I was out seeing Anders and Hansigne today, to talk to them about Kay. They're having a bad time of it. As I sat and noticed all the gaps in Hansigne's teeth, I came to think about you, and how, even with all your plenty, you were tired of it. You hardly know why, but you often wonder how you could slip out of it in a nice way, so that Frederik wouldn't be too sorry about it."

"Is that how you thought about me?"

"No, I'm not telling the truth; I've just thought about it now, but I'm like you myself, so take no notice of what I said."

"But I do! What you don't know is that I can't do anything for anybody unless I'm told how to do it. I daren't do it myself, because I'm afraid of people and covered with shame by them. I feel it obtrusive; it makes me appear better than I am, and hurts them! It's almost an obtrusion to live, Johannes! I'm almost sick with shame when I try to do a little for someone, and consequently there's no one who bothers about me!"

"You aren't getting much good out of looking at the stars."

"Standing here like this, I could bear the whole truth, Johannes—could bear to hear you say that you don't really care the slightest bit for me! I only pretend that you do. No one does really, except Frederik, perhaps, in his poor little way: he has to have someone to cry over his trifles! I am, as it were, two persons: the one you will have, but not the other. If I could only have children—a child!"

"Shall I tell you about the schoolroom?"

"Yes, tell me."

"Really it's a long story and begins when I took a drink or two this morning on an empty stomach. That's why I came to behave as I did in church."

"I was madly infatuated with you."

"Then the Devil has sex, but we knew that, and I won't discuss that now—another time, perhaps. Afterwards I sat in the schoolroom and thought how much I had acted the cheat, how I was in fact an absolute impostor. I had deceived everybody and everything, and you know it. Then the schoolroom seemed to open up. Yes, it opened up! I can't describe it in any other way. I came into it really for the first time, and the schoolroom answered for me and forgave me as far as it was concerned. Now I belong there, my dear, and will make my home there as long as I can. I am a prisoner for life!"

"Are you glad to be a prisoner?"

"Yes, I think so; and now I've told you about it: I don't usually tell anyone anything."

"Thank you, my dear! Shall we go in now? Then their suspicions won't ruin the moment. We'll go in now and dance!"

In the hall, Valdemar and one of his friends had already begun to play their concertinas, and a lot of the older folk were on the floor. Beery, burning, copper faces! Closed, Madonna faces, with enigmatic lips! Look how each of the older women becomes a Mona Lisa while she dances! Smiles that are enigmas! The soul turned towards far distant, long-forgotten memories. The room booms, the huddle roars like a maelstrom, and up from the depths is whirled the stuff of life's dreams; fair, beautiful, dead moments come again, come once again!

And look, there is Annemari with her Alexander! The others hop and buzz around, but they glide over the floor like a lithe, twofold creature. A lovely couple indeed! But she and Oluf were beautiful together, unknowingly they brought color when they were together. Now she is different; she has tuned herself to a more grayish, bolder lover. There they glide, enchanted, interwoven, immersed . . .!

"He's the only one who has danced with her, others never get the chance!"

"Well, they are young!"

"Are you reminding me of my age, Johannes?"

"Fairy Queens have no age! Come, we will show them!"

"Yes, come, my dear! Fast and furious!"

When the dance was over, Rigmor shouted: "Ladies' choice!" She walked over and curtsied low before the engineer; Annemari was looking round. I left the hall and went in and sat at the table where they were one short. As the cards were being shuffled, Annemari arrived.

"Are you engaged?"

"Yes, you must excuse me, Annemari."

"I should like to talk to you about Tom—I've just heard about it."

So I had to excuse myself at the table and go with her. She said she would go home and see to Tom, so she fetched her coat and we went out into the yard; I told her what she wanted to know about little Tom.

As we reached the avenue, she said: "Shall we go round to the ramparts? I've been home and seen to Tom—naturally I went home as soon as they told me; shall we go this way?"

But I stopped and said: "I'm not sure that it's quite proper for a young lady. It wouldn't be right, in the opinion of an old gentleman who smells of lavender. Besides, your partner and I are no longer friends!"

"So I understand," she said in a peculiar tone, "and I should like to know what it is Harry can have done to you."

So we turned along the narrow path to the ramparts, and

I said: "Your friend has done me a service, and I'm truly grateful. He has told me some splendid home truths."

"I hope it was the truth," she said.

"It was a bull's eye, my girl!"

"And you couldn't bear it?"

"No, I took offense, my dear."

"I don't know what to believe," she said.

We walked on.

"I think I hate her, really hate her!" she declared.

"If it's Rigmor you mean, it's a pity," I said, "for I like her!"

"She has always humiliated me," said Annemari, "as she did just now in the hall."

We were approaching the little dark mound of the ramparts.

"Well, Annemari," I asked, "should we do it?"

"Do what?"

"Run away together, you and I?"

"You joke about everything," she retorted.

"It brings its own punishment," I said; "It's only in fairy tales the jester comes off best."

She put her arm in mine as we climbed the slope, and said: "Perhaps you don't care to tell me fairy stories any longer, but I should like to hear you tell me one, just once more—or will you tell me now why you really came to Sandö? You once promised that you would!"

"It's an ordinary kind of story, my girl," I answered. "You women always imagine that there's a love story behind every move, but it can be much less romantic; it could be that a man wasn't equal to his job, for example!"

"I don't believe that!—Look how they are reflected in the water!"

"Yes, they are constantly reflected."

"You promised once to tell me about Betty, the girl you got the necklace from."

"She was called Birte—the town treasurer's daughter—we were in the same class together. And it was through Birte that my heart was handled like a codfish from Lofoten; it was cut up and laid out to dry on the rocks, a laughing stock for everybody! But we were only young. Later it was just as bad for the others, many others, for Birte was pretty. Yet for a time, a whole year, I was in the seventh heaven of delight, because it was Birte and I, and I was studying literature, too. One day she sent me one of those nice little letters women can write. There was another, a common friend, older and more dashing than I. The bright bird flies swiftly, comes darting. Birte broke with me and I broke with my academic studies and went off to a training college. Later, ten years later, Birte's husband came as clerk to the magistrates in the town where I was teaching. I had perhaps forgotten Birte, but now we often saw each other again. The gilt had probably worn off their marriage, and off Birte too, perhaps. One day I said to her: 'Birte, you have lines round your eyes.' She looked at me like someone on the point of drowning. 'Birte,' I said, 'you are beginning to look beautiful now.' After that I had to be more careful; in fact I left the town shortly afterwards."

"Why had you to be careful?"

"I'm surprised you ask! Her husband, children, and so on."

"That was noble! How generous of you!" she declared. "But you should fight!"

"Fight!" I exclaimed. "How fight? You young folk like these high-sounding words."

"You did wrong, Johannes."

"On the contrary, everything is fine, at least it was the

last time I heard anything. The husband is fine, the children are fine, Birte is fine, and I am fine! Naturally her husband was a bit scared, and naturally Birte was rejuvenated. Perhaps she thinks I am a bit of an angel, but then just as thin and vegetarian as one imagines an angel to be. Her husband remained her husband on earth."

"It is cold," Annemari complained.

We turned and began to walk back.

"Johannes, what do you sit thinking about when you are alone?"

"Mainly about the poor wages a teacher gets," I replied, "and I have my domestic anxieties. Now I've engaged a housekeeper, Elna from the inn, to begin in May. I have my small worries, you know. But often I sit and think how handsome you were, you and Oluf, the time you came to the school in the dark."

She stopped and almost yelled: "Always the same! You know how you hurt me by always mentioning his name! If you could only lose your head and say something else!"

"My dear,' said I, "it is only a second ago I lost my head."

I took her back to the door of the Headlands and then went home.

X

MONDAY came.

The boat came; and Oluf came!

In the morning I didn't get out, as I intended, to look for woodcock in the copse with Pigro. From the middle of March until the migration is at its height, we are usually out every morning at dawn, and usually in vain, for it is an unpredictable bird, but the walks one takes at daybreak are never wasted.

I was too much out of sorts and had no fancy for it this morning.

It was after noon before the boat was sighted. We heard that it had had engine trouble on its way to Tulö on Saturday. We were impatient on our island, and the schoolchildren were restless.

People had used Sunday to write their letters. The little post-box outside the school was full, and during the morning I had a lot of interruptions from people who came inside with their letters and parcels.

They were going to ring to me from the quay when the boat was sighted. It is coming from Tulö Sound, in the northeast, and won't be seen from the schoolroom. From here I look only on to the drenched fields and out over the gray, foggy sea. The wind was southwest to west, it was blowy, sleety weather, and early this morning there were two or three short snow squalls, which had turned to slush on the ground.

Now and then I went from the schoolroom into my own room to look out from there. At other times, I've not been able to see anything but my garden, a true picture of my

161

life's failings, and then the dark spruce trees beyond. To-day was their Waterloo. Anders had come at seven o'clock to fell them. By lunch time so many had fallen that I could stand in my room and see right out into the clayey world—the fields over towards the black trees of the Head-lands, and the open sea and Tulö in the north. Two hours later the second line of guards had fallen: the sound lay open and desolate to the northeast. In spite of the raw air, one could glimpse in the far distance the church spire and water tower of the town.

Today I was not without my surprise for the children. I'd hung on the wall the large, clear map of Sandö, the engineer's gift to the school. I made a nice little speech about the donor, and the two school editors composed a few lines about the occasion for the "Sandö Times," the wall newspaper which hangs beside the door. This newspa-per records the island's news: the catches made by the fishermen; the sowings and harvests; the weather and mi-gration of birds, and whatever else happens. In the last few weeks there has been little to record. An old notice hangs on the board, its drawingpin turning rusty. It was put up early in February. The editors hadn't shown it me before-hand. Written in large block letters and with crosses round the edges, it read: "Saturday morning, 1st February, the cutter *Klyden* of Sandö blown up by a mine, out towards Gysand. Erik and Anker died."

Erik's son was in school. He read it with large, quiet eyes, and I got the impression he thought it ought to stay there.

A useful, beautifully drawn map of Sandö, showing the scattered houses where people live. The island isn't round, it looks almost like a wooden clog, with the toe to-wards the east, its point the gravel spit where the shelduck breeds. A little south of the spit lies the quay, whence a road runs for the two miles westwards across the island, first passing the school, and then through the village, and out between Western Hill and the Sand Hills, till it ends in a cart track in the heather over by the little storm-tossed copse where the woodcock swoop down. From the village a road runs northwards to the Headlands, and another southwards past Oluf's mother's house, turning west between the coast and the plantation, and on towards the church.

Only in one place can you stand and see that you are completely surrounded by water, that you are really on an island; and that is on the top of Western Hill. There are many places on the island from which you cannot see the sea, and where you could well believe yourself in the middle of a continent, with immense stretches of land in all directions. When I first came to the island I often sought out these places.

The map gave us many problems to work with in school, and we tried some of them, but the children were too restless.

When I had let them out at dinnertime the maid from the shop brought my dinner over. I had had this arrangement about my meals for many years. As I sat eating my meal, I heard a car outside—it was Frederik, of course.

"I see you are felling those fine spruce trees!" he exclaimed.

"My lord does not approve?" I said. "I must admit I haven't looked up the school regulations to see what they say about felling the trees."

"Really, you ought to have let the parish council decide the matter," he protested; "there was no immediate hurry!"

"It was a matter of life and death," I answered.

"No matter what the reason was," said he, "it would

have been better had we been asked. We would certainly have given it favorable consideration."

"I won't tell you to go to blazes," I answered. "On the contrary, I will send to the government of this deaf island a respectful application. I will apply for permission to engage as domestic servant a girl who is expecting her confinement in the autumn, and for whose child neither I nor the well-known rake of the island is responsible."

"Is it me you are being sarcastic about?" he asked, trying to bluster as well as he could, for after the previous night's party his eyes sat a little wrongly in his head. Frederik couldn't bear any allusion to his debauchery, however slight it might be.

"Who is she?" he asked.

"You will see in the application," I replied; "but you look as if you had just been in a battle."

His fine brown head had a moldy green tinge.

"I'm as fresh as a spring herring," he said, "even though I've had only a couple of hours' sleep. But I could tell you something!"

"What, about the three pennies in the accounts?"

"I found them this morning!" he answered; "I dreamt where the mistake was, and my dream was true. You had written a figure so badly that I took it for a four instead of a seven."

"Be sure your sins will find you out," said I. "You must forgive me, I do nothing else but make mistakes these days."

"You should get yourself a woman in the house," said he; "a man shouldn't live like a monk! To the devil with being an ascetic!"

"I have to be an ascetic, with the wages I am being paid for the job!"

"No, it's up to yourself," said Frederik; "show yourself man enough! When I see a nice girl, I come straight to the point. If there's an opportunity, I get hold of her. It's a deadly sin not to do it, parish clerk! You're in need of some rules of behavior, I think. It may be you haven't sufficient attractiveness for women, at least that's what I understand from Rigmor, but you have the devil's own gift of speech and you should make use of it! But here, I must see Anders! He must get off home in time to help to put Kay into the car. The boat is expected in an hour and a half!"

"You are going to take the boy over to the sanatorium, then?"

"Didn't I say that yesterday? No, I said Tuesday, perhaps. But it's better today. There'll be a hell of a fuss getting the car over now! But if I have the sick boy with me, they can't very well refuse. I have an urgent bit of business to do as well. I must see the company and the other interested parties before this engineer does any harm! His opinion about our lime project is far too pessimistic, he might upset things. He hasn't made the best use of his time here, he hasn't tackled the job properly!"

"And now you will make trouble for him?"

"I'm never ashamed of what I do," answered Frederik, and off he went again.

At half past one the news came that the boat would be in within the next half hour—I'd already seen it from my window. Anders was chopping away like a madman outside: three trees were still standing. If he fells them all before the boat arrives, Kay will get better, so fiercely he goes about it. In a short while he has to go home to help to pack his sick boy into the car. I have no idea what hopes there are that Kay will ever come home again.

Folks flocked past the school, on foot, on bicycles, on carts. It seemed as if the whole island was going down to meet the boat.

Finally the postwoman who delivers the letters and newspapers on the island arrived. I let the children out, but got hold of one or two of the big ones to help the woman and me with the mail.

On our way down to the quay I saw a flock of titmice flying in cheerful small arcs through the blustery weather; and as we stood I heard a blackbird squalling in a garden, a magpie chattered, and some partridges came scurrying in. I nudged the boys and told them to look up into the sky. At a giddy height a flock of migrating buzzards flew inland. Wheeling and circling up there these birds of prey have the proper perspective. How small everything down here must appear! Here it is black with people anxiously awaiting the spring boat. A colony of ants! Over there, in the shelter of the boathouse, stands Annemari by herself—and here stand I. While out there, in the prow of the boat, stands a man, a big, tall man. Yes, here we are! But seen from up there we are all ant-size, with ant-size problems, ant-size complications.

Yes, Annemari is here, alone, standing in the shelter of the boathouse, hiding her chin in the collar of her coat. I didn't see her when I first got here, she must have gone straight past me without my noticing. She wants to talk to Oluf alone, perhaps. We stood here once before and waited for him—she had to have someone to support her then—and Oluf hid himself below deck. This time he is standing in the prow, looking towards the island. He is coming home to do a bit of fishing, to sit about on a bench, and to play his violin sometimes.

The water is rough; drifting ice still lies below the surface, and now and then heels over in front of the bow of the boat.

It is only a few ship's lengths out now. People begin to call out.

I turned to the postwoman and said: "I've just remembered something I ought to have brought. You and the boys can see to things. If there are a lot of parcels get one of the men to help you. If you see Oluf, tell him I'll be seeing him."

I walked back to the school, went to my room, and helped myself to a stiff one. There, on the shelf, lay Annemari's letter to Oluf. It was comical—the envelope was crumpled and black at the edges from lying in my pocket.

Anders had gone home, he had felled them all, the trees lay like fallen soldiers. The garden is no more a closed world of dreams; now I can see the north side of the island, lying bare and soiled before me, and the Headlands beyond, like the island's dark womb.

Time passes, and then I hear the outer door open and something heavy is dumped into the passage. The door closes again. I go out and see the mailbag and some large, heavy parcels lying in a heap on the floor. There is only one man who can carry all this in his arms. I tear the door open.

Oluf is outside the gate, walking away; he turns to salute me with a finger to his cap, then he is lost behind the hedge. Of course, he must go home to see his mother first; that's understandable—it's natural.

I go back in and, passing the mailbag, give it a little kick, then a real good kick! I settle down in my room again.

A little later the postwoman and the boys arrive, and we begin to sort the mail, which the boys will help to de-

167

liver today. We sort it on the long table in the passage. There is nothing for me except the newspapers for the last six weeks. It will be nice to sit with the old newspapers, there is something redeeming about months-old news, like the sins of people past and gone.

But there is no letter, not a single letter the whole winter. Yet who can I expect to write to me? Seven years are too long to remember. What matter, letters are only a nuisance!

But there is a little parcel! Let me see: from the bookseller, a little book I ordered in January; and look, they've sent the wrong one! I already have this collection of poems. This little book has been lying about for months, thinking it was on its way to a good reader! I shall keep it; a man can do with two copies of a good book: one to carry about with him in his pocket, while the other goes in his collection in the bookcase.

The postwoman and the boys have gone off with the light post, leaving the heavy parcels for folk to collect for themselves. I lounge again in my chair and stare out. "Now, now, Pigro, you are fidgety! Lie down, Pigro, you are too restless!"

Time creeps by. At last! The outer door opens; I keep to my chair; a dull knock of heavy knuckles. "Come in!"

"Oh, it's you! Welcome home! Sit down. You look a bit thinner about the face, I think. How are things going?"

"Oh, so-so!" he says, and sits down.

Oluf is not so big as I remember him; he seems a little quicker now. He's filling his pipe from my tobacco barrel.

"By the way!" he says, and pulls a little parcel out of his pocket and lays it on the table. "It's for you! Not that it's anything special."

I open it. It's a new pipe, and I walk over to the window with it and stand there examining it carefully—a strong,

168

reliable pipe of good make, the bowl is beautifully turned and finished.

"You needn't be ashamed about giving a pipe like this to anyone," I say, standing with my back to him and examining the pipe carefully in the light.

"Well, Oluf?" I prompt after a while, drifting back. Annemari's letter lies under the cartridge-case on the shelf; I take hold of it, but put it down again.

He lights his pipe, looking at me with searching eyes as he puffs the smoke out. Then he says: "Look, Johannes, there's something I've been keeping up my sleeve all the time! When I went over to the mainland in the autumn, it wasn't only to make a bit of money; but I didn't want to say anything about the other—thought I'd wait and see how it turned out first. I've been to school over there—a bit of navigation and radio, and that sort of thing—and I'm going back again!"

"And what then?" I ask. It is beyond me.

"I might be able to take a boat, up near Iceland," he says.

"Really!"

"I've had a look at several," says Oluf, "and it looks as if it may be possible. It would have to be a large cutter, and we should have to get a State loan on it—one or two of us would have to put up something ourselves. What do you think? Mother wants to put some money into it. I had an idea she might, and in fact had half counted on it, but I didn't know for certain. It's not more than half an hour ago I got to know; she has some money over in the town, left to her by her family; she has never touched a penny of it and will put it into the boat."

"And you will go out into the North Sea?"

"Yes, and farther up."

"Really!" say I. I can't understand it, I think to myself.

169

"Look," say I, "here's a letter for you. I guessed you would be coming home on the boat, so didn't send it with the post, and now I've nearly forgotten to give it to you."

"It's Annemari's writing, isn't it?" he asks calmly.

He doesn't tear it open, but takes out his pocket-knife and slowly slits it open. I walk over to the light and look at my new pipe.

A little later Oluf says: "I had thought of staying at home for a fortnight, and wondered if I could come to you for some mathematics—it hasn't been my strong point."

"We can certainly manage that," I agree, "and if you have any difficulties of that sort in future just drop me a line—I'll soon get you going."

"I'm not used to it, I suppose," says he.

"Well, have you read the letter?"

"Yes, it's all right."

"What is all right, Oluf? But then it doesn't concern me, I suppose."

"It's all settled; I talked to Annemari, you know, a little while ago."

"Well, and what about it? I suppose it never occurred to you, my boy, that I, who have known you both so well, would be interested to know what has happened between you?"

"Only what had to happen, Johannes. We each go our own way. I've expected it for a long time, but I didn't think I ought to do it."

"Well!"

"I'm starting afresh. It's no good going on with something that I'm not cut out for, but I have only good to say of her; and she has a better head than I, if only she uses it now."

"What do you mean by that?"

170

"Are you playing much?" he asks, turning to the corner where I keep the violins.

"Rarely," I answer; "when a man is alone he loses the desire. But look here, Oluf, you could sit and play a while; if anybody comes for a parcel you know what to do—I have one or two money orders I ought to deliver."

He already has the violin under his chin, he looks up cheerfully with his head on one side, looks at the bow, and says: "Fair wind!"

I close the door of the room calmly after me, but I leap across the passage. Pigro wants to come, but doesn't get the chance, gets his paw jammed as I close the outer door, and starts howling inside. I beg your pardon, Pigro, but you must understand!

I run across the garden and off down the road—folks will stare if they see me, the parish clerk, come running like a wild man!

A car comes swinging round the bend, it brakes; there's nothing I can do, I have to stop.

"It's devilish busy you are, Nimrod!" calls Frederik from the car.

"Telephone message!" I pant.

Kay is inside. Now he is off to the sanatorium; he is packed well in and they've arranged the seat so that he can lie down if he wants to—I see it all crystal clear, though my thoughts are elsewhere—and at his side sits Hansigne, poorly dressed. She smiles with gaps in her teeth, but she would rather cry. Kay, too, smiles, and his eyes say that he expects something of me. Yes, I know, my boy, I ought to go with you to the quay, I really ought.

"Get better, Kay! I shall remember about the books! About antiquity, isn't that right? And remember you have to come home and help me to do some research on Sandö! Good-bye!"

171

They drive off, and I begin to run, carrying with me the disappointed look of a boy. "Antiquity!" Stuff and nonsense! "Research on Sandö!" Fiddlesticks!

Everything is at stake for me now, my boy!

I tear through the door at Höst's. There is a commotion in the house, I can see. I run straight into Mrs. Höst, who bristles with all her feathers.

"Dear me! dear me!" she cackles, and throws her arms round me. "Thank goodness you've come!"

She says it so nicely, this madly bewildered, fondly shameless woman, she's a lovable soul; I squeeze her and she loses her breath. I'm so overcome by a sudden, tempestuous confusion of joy that I kiss her.

"Where is she?" I ask.

Then up the stairs I go to the first floor. I try to control myself and go slowly, but I feel as if I have no weight, a wild feeling of joy has neutralized all gravity.

The door stands open, and I know it is her room, though I've never been here before. I am aware that it is terribly untidy, but I don't see it clearly. I see Annemari; she is sitting in front of a mirror combing her hair, that thick, dark hair, her eyes of black velvet, her mouth like a rose hip.

She sees me in the mirror, our eyes meet, and thus we look for a long time.

Then she nods and I begin to laugh. I lean against the doorframe, nod back, smile, and Annemari smiles, at first uneasily, then full and beaming.

On the drawers at the side of me lies a packet of cigarettes. Though I rarely smoke cigarettes I take one and light it. Her room is very untidy and two suitcases lie gaping wide open in their fullness. Yes, of course!

I am a bit surprised by it, and although I still have this light, intoxicating weightlessness, I have seen it and understand. Our eyes meet again. Yes, I see it. It is not the same

Annemari of yesterday and all other days. She mirrors an event; there is a tranquility of consummation and a cool sweetness in her eye. It has surprised and altered something in her. It has taken place; it has happened last night!

"Poor Johannes!" she says.

"Poor Pigro!" say I; "he was eager and got a paw jammed in the door."

"Ah! that was a pity, poor Pigro!" she says. Look, she has tears in her eyes! For Pigro or for . . .? No matter, they are just tears from the fullness of the moment, tears light and volatile as ether. It is the affluence which is touched by a dog's paw, by a loser who stands at the door.

"Pity!" she says, and is moved in a way that is not like Annemari—melting. Ah, yes! It was a tender, touching picture to take with her—the weeping friend, the weeping loser at the door. And there will come moments in the future, moments more mundane than this, when it will flood the memory with sweet sadness; but these she shall not see. "Pity!" she says. This she cannot say to me, for in this affair I have played an honorable part, a part according to the strictest principles. If I have lost, my loss is my greatest gain, more priceless than the reward of most love stories— but let me explain.

"Pity!" says a girl who ought not to. Until a moment ago, there stood between her and me one whom I could not injure—Oluf. Now she thinks herself new, changed, and confident, and she can say: "Pity!" But I can play a game, too! Annemari, you were like a wounded bird in the hand, and you encouraged the other to goad me. I was to show how much you were worth to me, by making a fool of the simple Oluf. But you were caught in your own net last night, and now you think yourself transformed after a night with a lover. I wonder, though? I owe him no consideration.

173

"You must bear with me, Annemari, for making up a story last night."

She looks at me through the mirror and smiles, but the smile is less expansive.

"I had to moralize, it was the circumstances in which I found myself," I say; "and didn't I tell you about a certain Birte? Yes, she was my sweetheart once, but a friend took her from me. Afterwards, I met them again, and I told you how I virtuously withdrew and left the town so that nothing should happen between her and me. A pretty story?"

"Really, what did you do, then?"

"There was no need for you to reproach me for not pursuing the right of love, or whatever you call it: I did it thoroughly. He had taken her from me—good! I came back and took my revenge!"

"Is that true, what you are telling me now, Johannes?"

"You can always rely on the bad things I tell you, my girl."

"But what happened? Why didn't you stay with her?"

"Stay? Perhaps she had overdrawn her account. Love's right, as it is called, says nothing about staying. The husband and she shared the children, and she got married again later, but not very happily, I imagine: I can't remember. The necklace, however, I had from her when she was young."

"Johannes," she said, turning towards me, "it was so beautiful and pure when you first came in here. We could have said good-bye to each other so beautifully!"

You thought it was beautiful, thought I, but it is finished now. Now I can hear his voice below, the voice of the winner. Why couldn't I have another day, even just another hour? It was an uneven game before, now it would be an even match. She is unsettled, she is almost forgetting that she is new and secure.

174

"Annemari," I said, "I never got round to telling you another fairy story."

"Harry is coming now," she said, with a sudden flush in her face. She turned away quickly, controlled herself, and was soon composed. She smiled towards me, but her eyes quickly withdrew. Just give me a day, even an hour, thought I.

The engineer was too surprised to be offended. He was a bit self-conscious. He is young, however, thought I, and he is certainly in earnest.

"Congratulations!" I said, and shook hands. "I hope you can forget that affair of yesterday. I had to come and say good-bye. When is the wedding?"

"Soon!" he answered. "At once!" he added, and smiled at her.

"If it is during the migration period," I said, "I will send you two or three woodcock. Woodcock isn't such a good-eating bird as many people say, not to my taste, and certainly not in the spring, but a beautiful bird for shooting. However, that was tactless of me—I forgot you don't like shooting."

"Don't worry about that," he said; "I was unreasonable yesterday."

"No, no!" I said, "you were dead right; if I hadn't been such an old, lavender-scented drawer, I would have seen everything differently. But I hope you will allow me, since you are plucking the flower of Sandö, to give your fiancée a little parting gift."

"No, Johannes!" she said, and stared hard through the mirror at the thin gold chain I held between my fingers, the necklace.

"Yes, my dear," I said. "I've always intended that you should have it when you went away. Let it remind you of Sandö. The island is like a circle; its shore is a chain, too. Hang it round your neck, Annemari."

XI

LATE on Monday afternoon.

"Can you hear someone chasing the ducks over by the barn? Something must be disturbing them. You don't think it's Pigro?"

"It isn't Pigro."

"They can't stand being chased about, they are brooding. Listen! Are you sure it isn't Pigro?"

"It can't be Pigro."

"You don't trust anyone, yet you have implicit faith in your dog!"

"Yes, next to God, there's nothing I believe in as I do my dog."

"That sounds strange to me, coming from you, Johannes! Do you believe in God, then?"

"I don't want to: I resist, I fight back as much as I can, but I believe for the moment, because I cannot loose the bands of Orion."

"What do you mean by that? You must explain what you are saying, my dear."

"It's only a quotation from the Book of Job. Job's God says to him: 'Canst thou bind the sweet influences of Pleiades, or loose the bands of Orion?'"

"Yes, but what do you mean by it, Johannes? I don't understand you. I think the longer I live, the more senseless life becomes."

"That's just it, my girl!"

"I don't understand it: it has slowly lost all meaning for me—life, I mean. What does the word 'life' mean, even?"

"I have no idea, Rigmor! Ask somebody cleverer."

"I can content myself with saying 'my life, my own life.' I long ago discovered that it was meaningless, absolutely meaningless! I don't even know how it has been spent. I don't think about it very much, Johannes, I only notice it, such as it is. I amuse myself a little over what Frederik means to do. He's so ambitious, and how busy he always is! Why does he bother? I think to myself. And I don't suppose that Frederik has discovered a purpose in it, not even that it's meaningless; he has no idea!"

"Oh, yes, he guesses, perhaps! That's why he buzzes about like a fly in a bottle."

"No, I don't think he realizes it—yes, perhaps as a restlessness. But because he believes in it all, I think he's worth more in life than I. Even if—no, I won't say anything about him! He's like a boy, a little boy, Johannes, he needs someone to mother him. I never think any more about leaving him; perhaps that was senseless, too. So I stay here and look after the house and the servants, I think I'm good at that, but there's something meaningless in it all. There would be meaning if—but you wouldn't understand that; but now I think it would be senseless to stop doing it, to alter anything. I get up in the morning, not that it really matters; I see to the house, water the flowers, and see that no one chases the ducks and the geese, and that doesn't really matter; I kiss Frederik, I am kissed by another, and that doesn't really matter!"

"Not even when you get a new dress, my dear?"

"You fool! Of course it does!—if only someone notices a little that I look nice in it! Perhaps it's the same with the other. I suppose I've been lying about everything I've said. It does matter a little to me, I should think, just at the moment, but not really deeply within me."

"Do I not matter to you?"

"Yes! Kiss me!"

"But not really deeply within you?"

177

"Johannes, when you really think about it, don't you think that it's senseless lying here, you and I? What will it come to? You are not serious, and we have been careful so long; I think we have been careful for a frightfully long time, but there was purpose in that, perhaps. But today, there you were suddenly, with your gun; you were going shooting, you said. Shooting! I knew at once what it was!"

"I was only going out to see if there were any woodcock, Rigmor, nothing else; I called in here, and there you were, looking lovely!"

"Perhaps a woman looks lovely when a man is wild, and you were wild!"

"You are lovely!"

"My dear, my dear!"

"Isn't that somebody walking about in the room above?"

"It's only the maid who has gone up for some onions. No one will come here; besides, the guest room is always kept locked, and they didn't see us come up."

"Are you sure?"

"Does it matter?"

"Not when you say it like that."

"But Johannes, you must answer what I was asking before. Oh, I am happy to be beside you! We've taken care for such a fearfully long time that you became almost a stranger! But this is not serious to you, my dear, not really serious?"

"Yes, it is, everything I do is serious; it is all put down in the book. It will all be remembered, will come again, all of it."

"It is dreadful, but it isn't serious with you."

"Yes, it is! I say yes!"

"Johannes, it could never become a tragedy, so it can't be serious. It can always end in tragedy for people who take it seriously, though there can also come something strong and true from it."

"Who says this couldn't end in a tragedy?"

"I do, Johannes. It would be all the same if we were found out, that's what makes it so meaningless. Frederik sees nothing, and if he got to know, even if I were to tell him, he would just find it something to cry over. He would be a bit spiteful and begin to brag about his affairs with girls, but he wouldn't dare to be jealous and furious about it. To him it is fundamental that one should be broadminded. And now you! It isn't true that you mean anything by it, it isn't serious with you!"

"For goodness' sake, stop it, Rigmor! If you say that again, I'll go straight out and empty a No. 6 cartridge into my stomach; but first I would shoot Pigro; then this molehill of an island could tell a legend about the man who was serious!"

"Johannes, Johannes! Lie down."

"You women must have proof, bodily proof; words aren't enough, knowing isn't enough. A man must be able to cheat a trusting friend, one whom he looks upon almost as his own son, before he can make sure of anything."

"I don't think it's very nice of you to be so unkind to Annemari, Johannes."

"I wasn't aware that I was speaking about Annemari; besides, that affair is over, the account closed by a stroke of the pen—that is how it's done. But why this should not be serious with me, I can't conceive. Yes, perhaps it does seem humorous. A couple of hours ago I had to realize that I had lost the game."

"Johannes, we can tell each other everything. I knew it was you she cared for, that is why I gave her to you last night at the dance, when I parted her from him."

"I see!"

179

"I could never have done it, if you hadn't spoken to me the way you did on the terrace. I conquered myself."

"That was fine; you didn't understand, however. You failed to understand that I couldn't cheat under such a handicap; that a man can love strong, unbreakable rules, and love the cleanness of his loss, afterwards. I was the steadfast tin soldier who let all temptation go by. I couldn't deceive a friend; I lost, and went away with the empty hands of the loser. I had come a long way since my younger days, I thought. Yes, I was swept and cleaned. And then what happened? Half an hour later, the steadfast soldier was in bed with another friend's wife! What do you think about that for principles? Don't you think the ground rocks a little? At one minute we are on the top of the wave, and the next we are down in the trough."

"That is why I think this isn't serious with you, in the way I mean, Johannes."

"That's possible, my dear. You are so meditative, and I would rather not think."

"You must listen to me, you must! Yes, you must understand that you have destroyed something, Johannes. I have longed for you to come to me, and now, when I am left alone, life will become meaningless for me in earnest. When we stood out on the terrace last night, you spoke as though I meant something to you; you needed someone to whom you could talk intimately, and you chose me. It helped me; I found that I had something alive in me after all. Do you know what I thought, afterwards? I thought that perhaps I could begin again, if only someone would believe in me. Now, I thought, I will begin to live again. But Johannes, where are all those fine feelings I had last night? I can no longer find them in me. Today, you didn't come to be good to me as you did before, you came to

180

find a partner with whom you could be wild. You were wild and wicked!"

"I was."

"I hadn't expected you to come like that, not after last night. But I had expected you. When the two of them went home last night, I knew that you would lose. I expected you, but I expected you to come and grieve."

"You thought I would cry over three pennies?"

"I wish you had come to grieve."

"Thank goodness you don't say: 'Pity'! I couldn't bear that so easily; besides, you are lovely!—worth a thousand others!"

"My darling! I have waited and waited for you! I can't help myself when you speak like that, but it's senseless, my dear, meaningless, meaningless, meaningless! I don't mean anything to you. I thought I did yesterday, but now you have destroyed what you created then, something that was living. I can't help it, it is meaningless now, you've made it a lie. You are only wild and wicked!"

"Yes, you lovely Fairy Queen! You sweet, whimpering witch! I am wicked! You're a witch and I'm the Devil, so we can hold a witches' sabbath. You know, of course, how the witches and the Devil played with each other? How, once upon a time, they used to play in the spring, up on top of Western Hill? Should we do it?"

"Let me go, Johannes!"

"You don't want to do it?"

"Let me go! I don't know what I will do with myself afterwards."

"That makes it all the sweeter."

"Let me go! I have always loved you!"

"Really?"

"I didn't want you to know it."

181

"Don't cry."

"Johannes, I would never have told you!"

"No, my dear."

"I have said it hundreds of times—on the telephone and at other times—'I love you,' just to hide the fact that I did."

"Yes."

"For, once it was said seriously, it became a reality, and things could no longer go on being the same; a tragedy might arise, and I should have to make a choice, Johannes."

"Yes."

"So we can't slink about in dark corners together like this, and come out again as though nothing had happened."

"No."

"What are you lying thinking about?"

"If I may be humorous, I am thinking how easily I could stab myself in the back and get thrown out of school. I don't think I'm really fit to be there."

"But you said yesterday the schoolroom had opened itself up to you!"

"That is right, Rigmor, moreover I had built up a kind of philosophy, yesterday, a whole outlook on life which I could maintain; I determined to expect discord, emotional discord. And wasn't I right? Yes, thank you, but in a way that has blown my theory sky-high. I couldn't foresee a single thing, was blown about like a leaf in the wind. I can't have very good qualifications as an educationist! And that I've committed adultery with my neighbor's wife is not the worst of it, not in my eyes; but the fact that I did it to do harm, to destroy."

"You said before that you believed in God. Wasn't it disgraceful to say that here?"

"No, it was fitting."

"I don't understand that, Johannes. I daren't venture on a discussion of great problems with you, about the world, war, and the meaning of life; I have only my own life, and although my life has always been an easy one, yet it has become meaningless to me. How then can I believe in a God?"

"You must! For when you reach the limits of meaninglessness, you find that all is a battleground where two forces fight, and there isn't any no man's land."

A little while later, with my gun over my shoulder, I was walking with Pigro on the way to the copse, following the path that runs north of the Sand Hills, along by the low meadows. Thick clouds, heavy and angular as rocks, drove across the sky, with clean-washed patches between, fresh and bright. It blew a good deal but there was no more sleet. The sea lay gray-haired, as if a leviathan had just swum through it. I thought I could hear the oyster catchers out in one of the shining pools, but I couldn't see them. Four or five lapwings wheeled round above the dark fields, from which all the ice had melted away. I saw some light balls go rolling across the grass dike, and then take to the air; it was a little flock of plovers. Other flocks on the wing came beating in against the wind, turning at great speed over the fields. At the head of one large flock were several golden plovers; the rest were plovers and sandpipers, and the white bellies of the sandpipers flashed as they veered in the wind.

Some migrating wine-thrush had settled in the copse, and as soon as we came among the trees, Pigro took up stance. I let him go forward; the bird broke just in front of his nose and disappeared in a hurried, thrashing flight among the trees. Pigro scowled at me from the corners of his eyes, asking why on earth I hadn't shot. But I broke the gun, took the cartridges out, and hung it on a dry branch.

I ran back along the path, the dog jogging along be-hind me, his tail hanging. Pigro couldn't understand this.

It was nearly a mile along the low meadows and past the Fairy Dell, and as we ran all the way, I got very short of breath before we were at the Headlands again. I hur-ried across the yard, in through the kitchen door, and on into the house. Rigmor was standing in the living room sorting out some linen.

"Put that down . . ." I gasped. "Hurry! Rubber boots, your coat! Hurry!"

I was waiting in the yard when she came out; she had tied a light scarf tightly over her hair, and it made her head look small and fine, but there was no sign of color in her face.

"Come," I urged, "we must move fast!"

I trotted in front—no, Pigro was in front now, a long way ahead.

I turned to glance backwards—she was running behind me, looking as if she expected to see somebody lying mur-dered farther on.

I slowed down a little and said: "No, there's nothing wrong, Rigmor. I thought you'd guess—the woodcock has come! It is here! But for your sake I didn't shoot, I want you to be there with me, though we can take it a bit easier, perhaps. What time is it? Not quite half past five—yes, there'll be enough light for another half hour. It gets difficult in the wood when the light fails, but we shall be there in time. What do you think about it?"

She walked alongside and smiled a little sadly.

"My dear," said I, "you mustn't walk there feeling so sad over what we've said. I know it was a deadly cold dis-cussion, my girl, but it will be all right, you'll see. It's a good sign, you know, the woodcock coming! A sign from heaven! You may smile, but it's a mighty good sign! We must help each other; I can teach you a lot of things: it sounds damned conceited, but it's right that I'm a clever fellow at doing things for other people. We'll soon find a way for you to begin, you must do something worth while, create something, that is what you're longing to do. And you'll do it! You mustn't go around with an after-the-war mentality, finding everything senseless. I know I'm a big idiot, I know that, I know that! But come! We can't just drift! Look over there! At those light stones rolling about— they are plovers; now they're in the air! Yes, it's spring, my dear! I don't know what we shall do, what will happen with you and me. See, those with the pointed wings are sandpipers! And the big fellows yonder, with the black heads and black throats, are oyster catchers, they stand there gaping, like sailors in front of the Tivoli. No, I don't know what it will come to between us, I don't know. But perhaps that's the wrong way to look at it, a bad habit, perhaps. The whole of this delightful present-day civilization is founded on the idea of happiness, is operated by the pursuit of happiness. One should perhaps choose a more exacting principle, a sterner law. But who am I to say, Rigmor? I know nothing. I don't know exactly what it will come to between you and me, but I'm afraid we'll have many bitter hours, many bitter, sleepless nights. Did you notice the flash of light as they turned in the air? They're sandpipers still in their winter dress; they go farther north. Look over there! There are some sandpipers with black shields on their breasts; they are Sandö's sandpipers, they stay here! My dear, I can't say what it will come to with us. I can help you and advise you when you begin to do something creative, but it must be your decision what we should do; you must decide yourself: I'm not fit to do it, I'm wilful and sly. Look at those black and white birds flying out over the sea! Long-tailed ducks:

185

they are moving around at present; in a few weeks they will travel a long way towards the north! What is the meaning of life? Yes, one can buy a whole mass of ready-made explanations and dogma, but they don't work. Life can still seem meaningless, can look as if evil and destruction are the true principles of existence. Stop a bit! I must have a kiss! I must. What shall we do, Rigmor? What was it I was saying? No, evil is not the only principle in life, for every kingdom that is divided against itself is brought to desolation, and if evil reigned supreme, it would be divided against itself and must fall. Which leaves goodness! Incomprehensible goodness! Warmth, purity, and light! They exist in people. I have a mind to strip you, my dear. Yes, I'll do it! I feel myself very strong now. But what I will strip you of is not your clothes, nor your years, but your doubt, your distaste, your mistakes, your dabbling with life, your fear of people! And look! Here walks a fine, good girl at the side of me, a girl who shines, a lovely girl, you as you really are!"

She clung to me tightly and cried, and I felt very ashamed.

"You must bear with me," I said, "I talk like the wind that grows as it blows. The woodcock is to blame for it, yet I meant every word."

"Couldn't you cry over us?" she pleaded.

"No," I answered. "No!"

When we reached the edge of the wood where I had hung the gun, I tied a little bell to Pigro's collar, put the cartridges in the barrels, and advised Rigmor to keep close in behind me. The woodcock had sat very close before, and we might get the chance of seeing a sitting bird. She asked if I would shoot it and what I meant by saying that it sat close.

"Out of self-respect, one never shoots a sitting woodcock," I said, "and I've never been very ambitious to shoot a lot of them. Shall we agree to let the first one go without shooting? If it flies up, watch how the bird seems to hang almost motionless for an instant, over the wood. But 'to sit close'?—that means that dog and hunter can go very close to it before it flies up. The woodcock is a mysterious bird; sometimes it sits very lightly, and then, usually, they all do the same, and vice versa, but nobody knows why."

We advanced from the east edge of the wood. Pigro went forward carefully and not too quickly towards the first place the woodcock frequented, a spot he knew better than I. There was a place here beside a damp glade, but I could hear by the bell that it was clear. Pigro drew southwards to a sour spot thick with bracken, where we followed him with difficulty. The copse is not by any means forestry-controlled; the farms have shared it for a very long time, and during the war a lot of timber was cut without plan. There is a strong undergrowth of creeping plants, bushes, and small trees, above which tower very crooked trees, covered in fungi and other excrescences, and with very twisted branches. In some places the copse is a labyrinthine tangle, enchanting to the wanderer.

Pigro drew slowly forward, there were still no birds. Rigmor followed close behind me. Once or twice when I turned round to see her, she was standing looking back, as if she thought someone was following us.

There was not a sign of woodcock in this part of the wood where they usually are to be found. I was beginning to think that I must have had a hallucination when I saw a bird before, or else it had been a solitary visitor that had dropped from exhaustion.

During the morning, the wind had been southwesterly, with sleety weather and occasional snow-squalls. If it was feasible to think that some woodcock had come down dur-

187

ing the morning, while it was snowing, one ought rather to look for them in some other places in the wood. I called Pigro to me, and we went out of the wood and across the moor, round to the west end, the windward side, where the low-growing trees stood like men carrying heavy sacks.

We made our way in between some raspberry bushes. Pigro was ahead, and I stood still for a while and listened, for the bell had stopped ringing, and only the wind whistled through the tops of the trees above us. The thicket had closed around us and we could no longer see out over the sea to the west, but from the sky above us we could tell that the sun had set. A cold stillness grew over every-thing and there came a mysterious something between the wood and ourselves. Her eyes grew large and dark, as I drew her cautiously with me. We stopped; I thought I heard a clink of the bell. If it was true, Pigro was a genius! We crept round some young, round-shouldered beeches covered with tough old leaves. Pigro was standing a short distance from an old pile of brushwood with withered scrub in front, but I couldn't see the bird.

"Watch Pigro now," I whispered. The dog began to cir-cle the bird, drawing himself slowly backwards and creep-ing silently to the side. A short while later, he was crouch-ing on the other side of the pile of brushwood. We drew nearer.

"Can you see that thick, moldering branch in the mid-dle of the pile?—it is forked—the bird is sitting just below the fork, can you see its eye?"

"Yes," she whispered. The dark, liquid-like eye looked fixedly towards us.

"Let it go," she whispered. I whistled softly, and Pigro moved forward.

The woodcock flew up with a rumble; she gripped my

188

arm. The bird almost hung in the air above our heads for a second, then went away among the trees, flying fast in short, broken lines. It came out above the thick tops of the trees a short distance away, and against the sky we saw, for an instant, its long beak in profile and its wings thrown over it like a cloak. Then it was gone.

"How strangely still it is now," she said.

"What does Pigro think?" I said. "Does he think there may be another here?"

"And you think we should shoot it?"

"I'm beginning to feel very superstitious," I answered; "I feel a lot depends on getting you a woodcock today, but it will have to be soon."

We followed the bell into the depths of the wood. At last Pigro stopped and we moved forward. There were stout trees here, covered in branches low to the ground, making it difficult to shoot, and the dusk had gathered quickly in the wood. Pigro was standing near something which looked like a pile of battered copperware in the failing light—old bracken. The dog drew round again.

"Can you see anything?" I whispered.

"Yes," she replied, "it is moving—that way!"

I could see nothing, but I let Pigro go forward. The woodcock stormed up farther to the left than I had expected, a wildly flung shadow. There was a swinging shot, then stillness.

"Was it the bird that screamed so strangely?"

"Yes, it has fallen somewhere in there—dead; Pigro will soon find it."

We could hear the dog searching a short distance away, so we moved in the same direction. "Johannes," she said; "I too believe that one can!"

"One can what, my dear?"

"Begin!" she answered.

189

The dog came with the woodcock in its mouth, I took the bird and patted Pigro.

"How warm it is!" she said.

"Take it," I said, "it signifies a pact between us! Look at it early in the morning, it's too dark now."

XII

EARLY in April.

Pigro has died. Yes, he is dead, and now I have only God to trust in.

I don't know what caused it, but the dog started to ail something and his coat just went dead on him. I consulted all the books I had, and tried to doctor him, but he just got worse. I was sorry that I had not sent early enough for the vet to come over to the island, but I could see now that it was too late. So we went out for our last shoot together, though the season was over. We just went over into Bödvar's field to set little Tom's partridges up.

Little Tom never got to see the partridges I had promised to show him. I didn't tell you, Nathanael, Annemari took Tom with her. The engineer liked him and was glad to be his stepfather, and Oluf agreed and said amen to it. Can you really understand it? Yes, Oluf no doubt did the right thing for the boy when he agreed, but I doubt if I could have done it.

Pigro was lying in his box in a state of collapse as I took the game-bag from the wall and slung the strap over my shoulder. You should have seen him then! His dull, watery eyes! I took the gun and examined it carefully, holding it up and peering through the barrel. I cleaned it, and when I looked through it against the light from the window, the barrel shone as bright as the sky. I carefully chose two cartridges, polished the nickel caps, and placed one of them in the chamber. You should have seen Pigro then! He got up, wagging his tail as well as he could. We walked slowly through the garden, across the road, and into the thick

191

grass, but poor tottering Pigro was not able to make his long dashes across the field. The two old partridges and their brood of fledglings got up and flew down towards the dike, so I knew that Pigro's nose was no longer up to it. I carried the dog down to the dike, searched carefully after the flock till I saw a glimpse of one of them, and then set Pigro down. I don't know if he had the scent of them but he slowly braced himself up and stood beautifully. When I let him go forward he swayed as he crept towards them. I went to one side; the birds rose and I shot. Thus fell Pigro.

I haven't been out shooting since. Besides, it's not easy to get hold of a pup and train it, and even if I was lucky enough to get a good one it would never be Pigro.

But after all, he was only a dog.

Perhaps I can't afford to go shooting any more. It was certainly a luxury, costing a good deal, and I never sold what I shot, but more often than not gave it away to somebody. Yes, it was certainly a luxury, and now that I have heavier responsibilities than I had before, have more people in the house—we are three, now, to live on my salary—it can't be done. I was never a good economist, I had some small debts even before; now I have a few more. There was more furniture to be got, bedding and other things, for the rooms that had stood empty, and, of course, a woman couldn't be expected to cook with the few things I had in the kitchen.

It was last year in July that I shot Pigro, late in July, for Bödvar had mowed his barley, and since then I've never been out shooting. Actually, I've never been out shooting since last spring, when I shot the woodcock for Rigmor. That was in March; it will soon be thirteen months ago, and I am just as wise.

Perhaps you don't like such a sudden jump in time as

thirteen months, Nathanael? Well then, I had better confess to you that all I have written in these perishable notebooks, all that I've told you, I have written only recently, a year after it all happened. Only now have I written it. It's true that I began to write down the small incidents of last year on the thirteenth of March, the day we had the fog and thought the ice would break, and I heard the children screaming down on the shore. But it was only the first few dreary pages that I wrote then. I stopped that same day, when I went down to see to the children. I was too restless to go on with it after that, I couldn't do it.

Thus I have imposed on you, Nathanael, and it is perhaps for that reason I have written the words, "The Liar," at the top of each page of these notebooks.

On the other hand, it was perhaps necessary for me to make you believe that everything was told just after it had happened, otherwise I should not have been able to make it real to you, to give it vitality. Perhaps, too, a man couldn't have talked about his dog, about birds and shooting, if he hadn't all the time sat here with his little, dark secret, that Pigro was dead.

And there could well be other reasons for calling myself The Liar.

But what was it I was telling you about? I was speaking about Oluf and little Tom. Perhaps it wasn't so easy as it seemed for Oluf to let the boy go, for although he himself has never said a word about it to me, I can gather it from what his mother said. She remembers Annemari with hate, although she doesn't often show it, and I wouldn't call it a narrow hate, either, for she can just as easily speak well of the girl, now and then. It is obvious, however, that Oluf's mother has passed sentence on Annemari and she can never afterwards be acquitted. According to the older woman's opinion, Annemari was cast in impure metal.

She was one of these modern pleasure-seekers, a girl with a dream of happiness; she sought happiness, and that gave offense to Marie. Oluf's mother is law-abiding, she stands for the law, as her parents did, and Annemari took little Tom with her, away from the island, and that is unforgivable. Tom was of Marie's stock, and whether Oluf agreed to it, or even allowed it to happen, Marie doesn't know, or rather behaves as if she doesn't know. When hate shows itself in Oluf's mother, it reminds me of the fracture surface of a huge hard stone block; it will never change.

I believe Oluf missed little Tom more than he showed, for it is easy to see that he is very fond of little children, when he peeps into the schoolroom here. And Oluf is no longer so afraid to show it; he is altered. He will never be light-natured, but it was certainly a release for him when his affair with Annemari came to an end; the two women were almost strangling him. Moreover, he lost faith in himself: there is little doubt this happened when Niels and he sailed out and Niels was drowned. I remember it; I was standing with him down by the quay, just before they went out. Oluf stood looking out over the stormy sea, with a mad look in his eyes. I understood him. He is nearly choked by the women and his own doubts, I thought, and he wants to measure his strength against Death's; if he wins, he will become a man. I encouraged him; but had I, perhaps, hidden deep within me a quite different thought? I forgot about Niels, completely forgot Niels, and I left them, and they went out in the boat.

But Oluf has recovered, and he often looks in here when he comes home to Sandö with the cutter; then he always wants to play with the little ones, and I always allow him.

The baby is bawling away in the house. He has cried all the time I have sat here writing. I'm forbidden to go in and play with him to quieten him; I'm not allowed: if I started to do that, there never would be any peace, says the authority. He would be spoilt by it, she says, and he is going to be properly brought up, so let him cry himself out and learn to go to sleep. Ah, yes, there is a lot of trouble with such a little one!

I'm sitting in the schoolroom. The children have gone home two hours ago. The sun stands over the plantation and the lighthouse looks like a flame of fire. A fine day. Spring is in its full youth. Just less than a week ago, we were having awful weather; the spring fretted and cried, and the sea behaved as wildly as it did that speckled and furious April day, ages ago, when Niels was drowned.

There are flowers in the schoolroom, cockscomb, marsh marigold, saxifrage, and others. They stand, each in its little glass, on the cupboards and shelves at the far end of the room. There one can best see their colors against the dark wall. I have had great difficulty in sneaking the small glasses out of the cupboard in the house, where my poor quarters stand clean and tidy now. I always used to use the glasses in the schoolroom here, but now it is almost forbidden by the authority.

The other day, the glasses with the plants in them stood on the window sill. There they are seen against the light and the fine shape of the leaves and stems shows clearly. But first they stood there for a day with paper hats over them, and you had to raise the hats if you wanted to see them. Yes, my old tomfoolery!

Today I have been out with the class of little ones to see where the flowers grow. We didn't touch the flowers on this outing, but began by being respectful to them, and why not show as much respect for a dandelion as for a minister? I have never yet allowed the class of little ones to pull a flower to pieces to count the stamens. I don't know where that foolish idea comes from, that one must begin

195

by cutting a flower in two to count its sexual organs. Systematization gone mad! No, first we learn to know them by their looks and how they are dressed, then we learn their names. Flowers, like everything else that means anything, must grow into our very language and become alive there, must be concerned in our lives, before we play the scholar, before we play at science.

But forgive me, I'm riding my hobbyhorse again.

Spring swells outside. The beach buzzes with birds, curlews amongst them now, but soon they will be moving on, most of them. The nights are full and heavy with migrations. I lie awake and hear them, and clench my hands.

The air foamed and frothed over the island for several days. Sandö was blurred in sea fog and vapor, while drift sand from the Sand Hills whistled against the window panes of my room, and the Headlands vanished from sight behind the driving sand. You will remember, perhaps, that my spruce trees have gone, and I can now see over to the Headlands. Bödvar lay on his stomach and spread out his arms and legs to hold down his fields, to stop them from being blown straight into the sea. Nobody could remember the like of it, and everyone thought that it was the end of everything. Then the hail came roaring like a cavalry charge across the island, and heavy downpours flooded the ground. No one had seen the like before. The lark sang throughout it all, now hurled away by the scoop of the storm, then back again.

Now all is quiet in the sky and on the earth.

The sun shining through the west window falls on the back of my head. It makes the papers lying on the table so dazzling. Here lie five full notebooks, "Sandö, 1-5." I've begun my description of the island, Nathanael, and believe what I've written is fairly truthful, even if not very much is worth publishing. It is a belated and heavy task

196

to collect and sort the information about our little island, and it will take a long time, many years, before it can be put together to make a reliable work, but it is a delight to do it. At first, I thought it was nothing but a great vanity on my part, and perhaps it was: it was an escape; but later I thought it my duty. And there is something cleansing in laboriously collecting the fragments of true knowledge. Perhaps that is why I have set the words, "The Liar," above all that I have written about my life in the other notebooks. For what I have told will sail past you and me, like clouds in the sky, loose and drifting, while the firm knowledge is like the stone and the turf which are found on the earth and remain here.

I've made a copy of part of my account of Sandö and sent it to Kay. Now and then I've had a little letter from him. His interest in antiquity isn't so strong now, but it may come again. His last letter lies before me, and in it there is a sentence I've thought a lot about: "I am not so well," he writes, otherwise he never complains. When I last went to see him at the sanatorium he looked a little better, and at least the doctors hadn't given him up. But Kay was almost nothing but eyes.

"I am not so well."

Others are well. Occasionally I get a letter now. I had three from Annemari, though she has all the world to think about. Yes, Annemari has the world and its great problems in her head now. By careful though quick thinking, she has arrived at exactly the same point of view as her splendid husband, fortunately! Two-thirds of the letters are written on that subject, and I hurry through them, but what she writes about their home, about little Tom, and about the baby that is expected, I read carefully. I began the correspondence myself. I knew that I'd frightened her by giving her the necklace as a parting gift, for wasn't it as if there were a curse with it? Later I wrote a few lines to her and her husband, about this and that on Sandö, about our little happenings here, and Annemari understood by them that I had changed my mind, and she replied with a nice letter, that I carried round in my pocket until it was no longer nice.

How are things otherwise on our island, my friend? Well, the pier by the quay is to be rebuilt with public funds, so the cutters will get a better landing place. Frederik, of course, is its champion; he is going to do something for the fishermen! But when it is finished, larger boats will be able to come alongside and load lime, so they say. Yes, and Frederik is now a county councillor and represents all the islands out here. Something is happening at the Headlands. Now that the spruce are gone I can sit here in my room and see over there; and at the Headlands, too, they have felled the trees, the dark, shading trees.

The baby has begun to bawl again, but I daren't go in. I am master only in my own room, and if the authority shows itself here, I shoot!

I've many a time cursed myself over the day I asked Elna to move into the school, so that she could have her baby. I've more than once taken a drop more than I ought to, for that very reason, otherwise I've been fairly careful. But I drank a lot just after the partridge shooting.

The baby has to learn to lie quiet. She's a determined woman, Elna, I will say that about her. I wouldn't stand her bossing me around, if it weren't for a certain reason, but Elna doesn't dream what it is that makes me hold my peace. No, she never thinks. That, perhaps, is a vice, too!

But it would certainly be a very different thing if Oluf came and wanted to go in and see the baby! Oh, yes, he could! No! I won't suggest anything about Oluf and Elna, just because I feel myself a little affected by it, and feel middle-aged and shut out.

But what doesn't it cost me! I can't afford to buy cartridges any more, but when can a man pour himself out a little glass of cognac to console himself, or sit and put crosses in the bookseller's catalogue? Never! And only because a little one has to lie there and scream.

But Oluf is slow. As it happens, there's very little I can say about Oluf that I haven't already said. It was that March afternoon last year, when I shot the woodcock for—well, for her. I don't think you were with me on that occasion, Nathanael. No, you seemed to disappear on the night of the spring ball, though I'd got used to talking to you; but at the dance at the Headlands I got round to talking properly with somebody, and you no longer existed. But—here you are again!

As I walked home from the wood that evening, after shooting the woodcock, I was alone. I walked up to the top of Western Hill, and with Pigro beside me stood for a long time on the big stone that lies on the top of the hill. Perhaps it is a sacred stone that has been used for sun worship: the rays of the morning sun strike this stone the first of all, and in the evening it is the last they light upon; or perhaps it is an old sacrificial stone on which they sacrificed the boar, or even made human sacrifice.

I reached the top while it was not quite dark, in those last minutes of the dying day, which the wanderer values as highly as the miracle of the dawn: you know, when space turns deep blue and the near is the distant, whilst the distant is drawn in towards you. You stand looking about you into the lapsing world, and hear that the wind can recite poems by heart. Now you see only the dark blue, and you watch the first flickering star being lit. Then the hunter knows that soon he will hear the whine of beating wings, the first duck; and he who has a burning wound cools himself in the stillness. In such moments, even he who always has doubt and unbelief like track hounds at his heels, realizes the divine as a power over him.

It grew dark. Far away in the cloud mountains of the west, a huge fire still burned. The sea lay dimly below.

It was the first time that I had stood here on Western Hill and realized that my fate was bound for always to this hill in the sea: not bound by a root, as are those who are born here, but struck into the island like a spear that is thrown from afar.

I stood on the sacred stone and thought: Here must I choose, here must I sacrifice! More I dare not say. I am grown too old to dare promise more than I know I can do. I can say yes or no; whatever else a man like me says is really nothing but deception. Yes or no. The time for flight is past, the dream is out. I can choose my fate, I can fight, but I cannot grow. I cannot turn back, but that we all know. Only the button-molder can remold. My feebleness and sin are great, for I know God's presence only when He strikes me hard.

But we are not all alike, there is another kind of person. There are those in whom the word, the incident, the emotion bring release; that change, turn green like plants brought out of the shade; that have growth in them, and if they love, they flower and fruit, even though they do not live happily. I believe that she whom I have wronged more than any other is such a person.

I am not like that.

However, Sandö has use for me, I thought, as the darkness gathered. The island folk no longer grow from their childhood, as they once did, in the recollection of their families and their country. There has to be someone to

200

teach them it now, even if he comes as a stranger among them, for he can see better than they can see themselves that the island must be conquered now, just as it was a thousand years ago.

I stood in the growing darkness and saw the island below me. Though small on the map, it has immense importance for a man, and here in the dark it grew weirdly strange. The island has an enormous capital of time in itself, time past and time to come, against which one man's age and memories are as nothing. The oldest legends hang on to it only by thin, fragile roots, and even they are best known by a schoolmaster recently come here. But even the legends are not so old as the mounds and the cairns. The language man spoke then has blown away, and so too, perhaps, will the language we use now, Sandö will then be called by another name. The flowers, the trees, the birds, the sitting hare, the pebble on the beach, will all have other names, and thus no longer will be the things we have known. Even that which we call our culture is perhaps only a season's fleeting flora, compared with the boundless ages and faithless unchangeability of the island.

The island lay like the body of a monster under me, and I did not imagine, as one often does, that I understood it from the bottom of my soul. It was now a monster that swallows people and consumes generations, so that all is forgotten. Even if, in the light of day, it has a form with which we are familiar, it has taken this day-form only because it has been overcome by the mind, bound by the use of language, and conquered by that culture of which we are all too skeptical. Thus I believe now that each generation must conquer the island, that it is vital to conquer it! To steal from its beauty is not vital but parasitic! It is vital to set plow in its soil and plow, and to set pen to paper to conquer it through knowledge.

201

Well, well, Nathanael, it all sounds very serious. I only mean that there is use for a schoolmaster on Sandö, one who will be here and nowhere else.

I wandered in the dark towards the church. I noticed that I was shivering slightly, and that Pigro was shivering too—the dog was alive then, you know—perhaps it was the cold. I thought I would go into church and see the stone head that some artist of the past has carved. It must be the head of Death, of Destruction, the head of Oblivion and Meaninglessness. It could also be said that the head had the face of the island, so cold and terrible it is when nature overcomes us. But this head, this Death, is placed in the choir so that Death gazes straight up at the symbol of the Resurrection, which the understanding cannot conceive. The idea of the Resurrection still holds firmly, sticking like a harpoon in the body of the island.

But when I got there I hadn't courage to go inside. Man is what he is. Instead I wandered round the churchyard, and got the idea of looking for the plot where I should like to lie among the other past people of Sandö. The jester never forsakes me! I chose a spot beside the wall that runs out towards the beach, then sat myself on the wall and Pigro jumped up beside me. There we sat.

Some while after, Pigro began to sniff and get restless. "Down!" I said. He lay down and I held him lightly. Someone came up the hill and in through the gate, walking heavily. He went round behind the church and I heard the steps hesitate, then stop, beside Erik's propeller shaft. A little later, he came past the tower and stopped beside Niels's grave. He stood a long time. Pigro trembled and shook.

He said something standing there. Said? No, it was a strange sound, not the sound that comes from a human being; but after a while he left.

I sat on for a while with the dog, then I sprang down and whispered a name to Pigro. He was off like the wind into the dark.

Almost in the center of the wood, Oluf stood waiting with Pigro.

We stood a while.

"Listen!" I said. A flight passed over.

"Widgeon," he said.

We chatted as we walked away. After a while I said: "I did wrong that time. You wanted to tell me what happened when you were out there with Niels, but I stopped you. I thought it best for you to feel it badly."

I expected him to say something, but he remained silent.

I thought I could help Oluf, and said: "No doubt you have often thought you were greatly to blame over Niels, and it's no good saying you are blameless, but there's another who is more to blame than you. I could have stopped you both, but I didn't, I encouraged you."

We walked on and I expected him to answer, but he kept silent. I tried again, but gradually I realized that it was too late. Oluf had made up his mind that he alone was responsible. It was too late, I had lost the right. So it is with so much else, too late! And all is remembered and will be remembered.

Yes, it is late now and we must part. I will tell you we have had a mild winter this year, and the ice didn't close us in. The sea birds have been very fat. I saw some Anders and Valdemar shot, but I haven't shot any myself. I was out looking at them through the field glasses, though. And now we are into April. Everything is early; I have heard the large curlew, and seen the wild chervil in the ditches. And now we must part, Nathanael. I am not allowed to write more, yet I am afraid to stop, afraid, I say!

Yes, I am happy here in the schoolroom. I think it is

very difficult to be a good teacher, but there are many happy moments with the children, and I work away at my account of Sandö. Elna's little one gives me a lot of pleasure, too. It might well end in Oluf's making up his mind, but I hope he will be slow about it, so that they will stay here a little longer. Yes, it has even come to that! When the nights warn me of my approaching loneliness, when I shall be alone with what I remember, alone with a powerful discipline, then I, like another Job, turn myself towards Him and grumble in my affliction, as one who would rather be cut down in a sharp, wild struggle than go with want festering in him.

Farewell, Nathanael! I let you go with difficulty. Until now I have pretended to be fairly calm, as if things were better, and in a way they are, for I am no longer a visitor here, but a man in his proper place. You must not be sorry for me, Nathanael. If you go away saying: "Pity!" you haven't understood me. Everything is as it should be. But the lovely spring can be painful. At times, when I look from my room over towards the place which once was hidden from me by the spruce trees, there seem to me only two solutions: either to go down there and take what some would call my right, or drink myself to death. I do neither.

I haven't seen her alone since the woodcock shooting. I could easily go over now and take her, and bring her here to my house, but it would never do. I would soon choke that which is growing in her, I know, because I nearly killed it once before. It was no doubt her I loved, but I deluded myself, and others too, that it was the other. I was fond of that game. But I know that she grows and will blossom into a fine humanity. She is different from me and I could help her only once. And now we will talk about it no more.

I recall that in Egil's Saga it is told how a man, many years after Egil's death, found a large skull in the ground. It was very heavy and abnormally thick. When the man laid it on the church dike and chopped at it with his axe, he could only make a white mark on the skull, though he struck it with all his might. It was thought that it must be Egil's skull. I think, hereafter, it must be the same with my lot in life. It is as God wills it. However great my anguish in the night, when I awake it has not bitten into my burden of loneliness.

QUARTET ENCOUNTERS

The purpose of this new paperback series is to bring together influential and outstanding works of twentieth-century European literature in translation. Each title has an introduction by a distinguished contemporary writer, describing a personal or cultural 'encounter' with the text, as well as placing it within its literary and historical perspective.

Quartet Encounters will concentrate on fiction, although the overall emphasis is upon works of enduring literary merit, whether biography, travel, history or politics. The series will also preserve a balance between new and older works, between new translations and reprints of notable existing translations. Quartet Encounters provides a much-needed forum for prose translation, and makes accessible to a wide readership some of the more unjustly neglected classics of modern European literature.

Aharon Appelfeld · *The Retreat*

Translated from the Hebrew by Dalya Bilu
with an introduction by Gabriel Josipovici
'A small masterpiece . . . the vision of a remarkable poet'
New York Times Book Review

Grazia Deledda · *After the Divorce*

Translated from the Italian by Susan Ashe
with an introduction by Sheila MacLeod
'What [Deledda] does is create the passionate complex
of a primitive populace' D.H. Lawrence

Carlo Emilio Gadda · *That Awful Mess on Via Merulana*

Translated from the Italian by William Weaver
with an introduction by Italo Calvino
'One of the greatest and most original Italian novels
of our time' Alberto Moravia

Gustav Janouch · *Conversations with Kafka*

Translated from the German by Goronwy Rees
with an introduction by Hugh Haughton
'I read it and was stunned by the wealth of new material . . .
which plainly and unmistakably bore the stamp of Kafka's
genius' Max Brod

Henry de Montherlant · *The Bachelors*

Translated from the French and with an introduction
by Terence Kilmartin
'One of those carefully framed, precise and acid
studies on a small canvas in which French writers
again and again excel' V.S. Pritchett

Stanislaw Ignacy Witkiewicz · *Insatiability*

Translated from the Polish by Louis Iribarne
with an introduction by Czeslaw Milosz
'A study of decay: mad, dissonant music; erotic perversion;
. . . and complex psychopathic personalities'
Czeslaw Milosz

Hermann Broch · *The Sleepwalkers*

Translated from the German by Willa and Edwin Muir
with an introduction by Michael Tanner
'One of the greatest European novels . . .
masterful' Milan Kundera

Pär Lagerkvist · *The Dwarf*

Translated from the Swedish by Alexandra Dick
with an introduction by Quentin Crewe
'A considerable imaginative feat'
Times Literary Supplement

Robert Bresson · *Notes on the Cinematographer*

Translated from the French by Jonathan Griffin
with an introduction by J.M.G. Le Clézio
'[Bresson] is the French cinema, as Dostoyevsky
is the Russian novel and Mozart is German music'
Jean-Luc Godard, *Cahiers du Cinéma*

Rainer Maria Rilke · *Rodin and other Prose Pieces*

Translated from the German by G. Craig Houston
with an introduction by William Tucker
'[Rilke's] essay remains the outstanding interpretation
of Rodin's œuvre, anticipating and rendering otoise
almost all subsequent criticism'
William Tucker, *The Language of Sculpture*

Ismaïl Kadaré · *The General of the Dead Army*

Translated from the French by Derek Coltman
with an introduction by David Smiley
'Ismaïl Kadaré is presenting his readers not merely
with a novel of world stature — which is already a
great deal — but also, and even more important, with
a novel that is the voice of ancient Albania herself,
speaking to today's world of her rebirth' Robert Escarpit

Martin A. Hansen · *The Liar*

Translated from the Danish by John Jepson Egglishaw
with an introduction by Eric Christiansen
'[The Liar] is both a vindication of religious truth
and a farewell to the traditional modes of extended
fiction. It is haunted by literary ghosts, and English
readers will recognize the shadowy forms of Hans
Anderson…and Søren Kierkegaard' Eric Christiansen

Stig Dagerman · *The Games of Night*

Translated from the Swedish by Naomi Walford
with an introduction by Michael Meyer
'One is haunted by a secret and uneasy suspicion
that [Dagerman's] private vision, like Strindberg's
and Kafka's, may in fact be nearer the truth of things
than those visions of the great humanists, such as
Tolstoy and Balzac, which people call universal' Michael Meyer

Marcellus Emants · *A Posthumous Confession*

Translated from the Dutch and
with an introduction by J. M. Coetzee
'Since the time of Rousseau we have seen the growth
of the genre of the *confessional novel*, of which
A Posthumous Confession is a singularly pure example.
Termeer [the narrator], claiming to be unable to keep
his dreadful secret, records his confession and leaves it
behind as a monument to himself, thereby turning a
worthless life into art' J. M. Coetzee